the Skinner's tale

CHARLES NICHOLSON

STACKPOLE
BOOKS

This is a work of fiction. Characters and events portrayed here are sole-ly the product of the author's imagination and any resemblance to actual persons or places is purely coincidental.

Published by
STACKPOLE BOOKS
Cameron and Kelker Streets
P.O. Box 1831
Harrisburg, PA 17105

Printed in the United States of America
10 9 8 7 6 5 4 3 2 1

First edition

Interior design and typesetting by Art Unlimited

Library of Congress Cataloging-in-Publication Data

Nicholson, Charles, 1946-
    The skinner's tale/Charles Nicholson
        p.   cm.
    ISBN 0-8117-1939-1
    1. Hunting stories, American—Alabama 2. Alabama—Fiction.
I. Title
PS3564.I276S59   1991   91-12867
813'.54—dc20   CIP

For Rachel

The following stories originally appeared in the magazines indicated. Each story has been changed to some degree.

"The Christmas Deer," *Sports Afield*, December 1986
"End of a Season," *Gray's Sporting Journal*, Winter 1987
"Long Upon the Land," *Shooting Sportsman*, Oct/Nov 1988
"Hunter's Home," *Game Country*, Nov/Dec 1988
"The Skinner's Tale," *Game Country*, May/June 1989
"Dry Fall," *Shooting Sportsman*, Oct/Nov 1989
"Lost," *Game Country*, Nov/Dec 1989
"A Deer for Cholly Dormin," *Game Country*, Jan/Feb 1990
"Gathering at the River," *Field & Stream*, December 1990

Contents

A Deer for Cholly Dormin

This was the early sixties. Thirteen different kinds of bad trouble were brewing around the country, especially in the South, but Cholly Dormin didn't have time for any of it. Too many troubles of his own, Cholly said, to waste time worrying about things like Civil Rights and Vietnam and Russian rockets in Cuba. He didn't like them killing the president, though, but that was a long way off, and right now Cholly Dormin had four aces and the jack of spades laying face down on the card table in the main room of Boss Bishop's camphouse down at Pineapple Bend, a place so far back in the River Swamp that after the middle of November hunters had to bring their own sunshine, Cholly said.

What Cholly Dormin was doing was trying to get the bummed-up buttplate off that old piece of a 30-06 British Mauser he called June Bug because he said it would get on a deer like a duck on a June bug. Boss told him if that was the case then Cholly ought to call the gun Duck, and then Mutt Binders said given the way Cholly had been shooting lately Duck did seem to be a better than average name for Cholly's old gun, but Cholly just kept on digging at the buttplate with a screwdriver and said he had a dog named Duck once but a gun had to have a woman's name. "Ain't that right, June Bug?" Cholly said.

What Cholly was doing was trying to get at the hundred dollar bill he kept behind that buttplate for emergencies, because he had already bet the rent money and all his pocket change when Queen Merry Walker bumped him a hundred and called. Queen Merry had drawn the three of hearts to fill a six-high straight flush but Cholly thought she was bluffing until the very minute he threw his wadded-up old silver certificate on the table and paid the price to read 'em and weep.

Old Boss Bishop said then that was undoubtedly both the worst luck and the best luck he had heard of happening at the same time since Blind Billy Benson accidentally killed two big bucks with the same shot and then asked the game warden to help him drag them out of the woods. Boss said that in all the years they had been having Friday night poker games before the last Saturday of deer season at Pineapple Bend nobody had ever before drawn four aces that he could remember, and for the man who drew them to get beat by a cook holding a six-high straight flush she made the hard way had to take some high-caliber bad luck. Sort of a reverse miracle, Boss said.

And Queen Merry Walker, who had played in every single one of those games since 1937 because her husband, Jericho Walker, refused to gamble with white people, said, "Un-huh, Old Boss. You sure right about that. And Old Queen can buy herself some tooths that fits now, and maybe one of those duck-headed walking sticks Mr. Rosenberg's got in his store. Lord knows Old Queen didn't expect nothing like this, Old Boss. This sure is some kind of miracle."

But Cholly Dormin said it was about what he had expected all along, laid his cards down easy and walked over to the fireplace to stand, drinking Boss Bishop's Early Times and staring up into the black glass eyes of the mounted head from the monster buck Boss's granddaughter had killed when she was all of eight years old. "Bull of the Woods," the brass plaque beneath the white hair of the buck's thick neck read. "Two Hundred Ninety-Six and One-Half Pounds. Killed With One Shot by Dianne Perril Bishop, Eight Years Old." and centered under all of it the date, "December 24, 1952."

Just thinking about that day damn near made Cholly Dormin cry. He had helped Jericho Walker drag that little girl's ungutted monster all the way from the Meat Stand, way back near the far edge of Cypress Slough, through the swamp and up and down over the low, sandy ridges to the River Road, where Boss could get in with his truck, then helped Boss and Jericho lift that huge deer with its twelve perfect points that Boss wrapped in old quilts and blankets so none of the tines would get broken off in the truck. Cholly had helped them lift that huge buck up into the truck and then rode in the front with Boss while Dianne and Jericho rode in back with the deer, Dianne staring at it but not touching any part of it or Jericho either, all the way into Garrison so Boss could drive slowly down Main Street, stopping every five or ten feet to let somebody look and listen to Dianne tell her story, until by the time they got to Rumer's Feed & Seed there were twenty or thirty men there to help hoist that deer up onto the scales to verify the weight and hear the story told one more time. Even after all of that, Cholly could still hardly believe the child had actually killed the deer; even though he had seen her shoot her grandfather's shotgun before and knew that Jericho Walker had been on the stand to help her see the deer, Cholly only truly believed that Dianne had killed that deer herself when Jericho at last got the deer gambrelled at the camphouse and began to skin it. Dianne had cried then, like the small child she was, and Cholly knew for sure then that the Bull of the Woods was hers.

Cholly looked around the room at the other hunters. Dianne, a beautiful young woman now and no longer prone to crying over the spilled blood of animals, was sitting at the card table with Queen Merry and Mutt Binders and her grandfather. Others were milling around, drinking and talking, when Cholly announced to anybody who might happen to be listening that he had expected to lose tonight. Said that ever since his wife's mother and her twenty-six cats had moved in with them this past spring things had been going from bad to worst. Cholly didn't say worse. He said worst.

But nobody was listening. There was so much talking and laughing going on among the ones not actually playing cards that Cholly just shrugged, took the bottle down from the mantle and poured himself some more of Boss's bourbon, then sat back down to play cards.

"Trouble, Cholly?" Dianne Bishop asked while her grandfather shuffled the cards.

"A little," he told her. Said that as best he could figure out from her letter, his oldest daughter Vera, "Y'all know Vera," Cholly said; Dianne and Queen Merry Walker nodded they did and Boss started to deal; Cholly said as best he and Dixie could figure out from her letter Vera was living on a cactus ranch in south Texas with two burnt-out preachers, a draft dodger and seventeen Mexican holy rollers. Said not only that, but just last week his old dog Duck went and got himself run over chasing a bitch Chihuahua that wasn't even in heat, and now his wife had come down with the flu so he had not even had one hot meal in over a week.

Dianne Bishop said, "Well, at least old Duck died happy," but Cholly just glared at her with his good eye and then looked back up at the fireplace before he told her he didn't really mind all that too bad. Said he had lost better dogs for worse reasons, even though he did believe old Duck deserved a little better than to end up squished flat on the side of Short Street with his little red chili pepper flopped out there for all the church women to fuss at Cholly about like it was his fault somehow. And Cholly said that Dixie had never been exactly what anybody south of Memphis would be likely to mistake for an outstanding cook anyway, and he could pretty well ignore his mother-in-law and Vera too as long as the two of them weren't in the same room together, which was highly unlikely right now.

"Are you going to play cards or talk, Cholly?" Boss said with about as much patience as a whistling tea kettle, but Cholly kept on talking. Put his hand down over his cards while he told them he did not even mind losing every last bit of cash money he had in the world tonight, as long as it was to a woman smart enough to make good blackbottom biscuits in a wood stove and lucky enough to draw to an inside straight in the bargain.

In fact, Cholly told them, and everybody in the room was listening now because Cholly was talking so loud, in fact, he said, he had actually kind of enjoyed being laid off the past few months, especially considering the fact that the government had been giving him back fifty-four dollars of his own money every week, and as long as he kept looking for work and didn't turn down any of the hundreds of job offers he wasn't getting he could draw his pennies and still hunt every single day of deer season, which he had managed to do so far without the distraction of seeing, hearing, smelling or even so much as feeling the spiritual presence of any buck deer with antlers longer than a snake's hind titty. That, Cholly Dormin said, he did mind.

The poker game broke up at midnight. Queen Merry grinned her big, half-shy piano grin and told them, "If any of y'all's going to want breakfast before you goes hunting in the morning, y'all are going to have to let Old Queen quit winners tonight." And Cholly, who by operating on limited credit and playing conservatively had managed to lose another eighty-seven dollars, told Queen Merry Walker that she might as well go on and get as much sleep as she could tonight because as soon as Jericho found out how good her luck was running he was going to have her sitting right behind him all night long down at Red Riley Fungo's barn just so she would be there to spit on his dice when they cooled off, and Cholly said there wasn't going to be any more night-sleeping for Queen Merry Walker until her luck changes.

"You right about that, Mr. Cholly," Queen Merry said, still grinning, getting up to leave and stuffing a big roll of bills with Cholly's hundred dollar silver certificate on the outside down between the double cannonballs of her bosom. "You sure right about that," she told Cholly as she left the table.

"Luck don't change that quick," Boss Bishop said. "Or that easy." The only way you could tell that Boss was getting a little tight was by the way he squinched his eyes up behind his Teddy Roosevelt glasses, his *pinch mes* Boss called them, so the sides of his moustache pulled back and showed his teeth. That and the fact he would say more than a half-dozen words together in the same two hours without even being mad at anybody.

"You sure right about that, Mr. Boss," Cholly said, mocking Queen Merry, who had already gone out to the little two-room kitchen that stood attached to the stilted old camphouse by a covered dogtrot and looked, in the moonlight, like some trailing, boxlike dingy tied to the stern of Noah's Ark.

Queen slept on a pallet there, on the floor near the iron, wood-burning old cookstove, slept there on hunt nights because she always had, because her mother had too. Neither of them had ever had any real, lasting good luck either, so Queen did not believe in luck. Queen believed in Queen Merry Walker and in the fine, sure and powerful eventuality of Amazing Grace, but very little else. One thing Queen Merry Walker knew right then, though. She was not going down to any Red Riley Fungo's rat-infested old barn to spit on any of Mr. Jericho Walker's bones, not unless he wanted to get whopped with a mop handle like he did the last time she caught him and that Sammaline Singletray trash together. Just let that old fool even ask, Queen Merry Walker thought as she drifted off into a deep, untroubled sleep.

"What you need to do, Cholly," Boss was saying, loudly, standing with his elbow angled up onto the mantle and drinking whiskey from a paper cup while Cholly Dormin poked at the dying fire, "is get out there tomorrow morning and kill yourself a Bull of the Woods."

"Yeah," Cholly said, poking at the red coals with the toe of his boot. "People in hell need ice water, too." The room was very quiet. Most of the others had wandered off to find themselves an empty bed in one of the half-dozen sleeping rooms off the main room where Boss and Cholly were talking now, but Mutt Binders and his half-brother Dan Steel were sitting on a bummed-up old sofa facing the fireplace and not speaking to each other over something as usual, and Dianne Bishop was curled up in an armchair with a springer spaniel in her lap and reading a book she had chosen from among the hundreds old and new in the recessed bookshelf covering most of the west wall of the big, cypress-paneled room. The book was Ernest Hemingway's *For Whom the Bell Tolls*, and Dianne was far away in Spain.

"Ice water my ass!" she heard her grandfather shout, hearing him as through a thick wall and then looking up. He was smiling, but only a little. Dianne looked at Cholly Dormin and watched him standing there, snuggling his toe into the coals as if he were trying to see just how much heat his boot could take without actually bursting into flames.

"Just a joke, Boss," Cholly said. Dianne was not sure exactly why, though she thought it had something to do with the fact that life had always seemed to deal Cholly Dormin one bad hand after another and Cholly just joked it off and kept on trying; she did not know for sure why, but she did know for sure that Cholly was one of her grandfather's favorite people and one of the very few men or women who had ever been welcome to hunt at Pineapple Bend any time they wanted and without having to wait to be specifically invited. Dianne knew too of at least three different ways Cholly Dormin had found to go broke, and that because of that a lot of people in Garrison considered Cholly a loser, but Dianne knew that Cholly didn't, and she knew her grandfather didn't either.

"It seems to me, Cholly," Boss Bishop was saying, "that the only way I'm going to be quit of having to listen to this slow, sad song of yours is either to shoot you at sunrise or take you out to find yourself a big deer to miss." Dan Steel and Mutt Binders got up and went out on the porch to be mad at each other, so Dianne and Boss and Cholly were the only ones left in the smoke-and-whiskey-smelling room.

"Maybe you better just shoot me then," Cholly said. Dianne could smell the sole of his boot burning, and when he turned his back to the fire she could see tiny wisps of smoke coming from the rubber.

"You ain't worth the shot and powder, Cholly," Boss Bishop told him. "You just make sure you're ready to go to the woods about four-thirty or a quarter of five."

Cholly had to sleep on the sofa unless he wanted to sleep outside on the porch, which he did not. It was cold outside, but he got woke up about two o'clock anyway when Mutt Binders and Dan Steel got into a fistfight out by the big artesian well and broke the pipe that brought water in to the camphouse toilet. He listened while Boss threatened to string both of them up from the game pole if he had to crap in the woods that morning, then Cholly couldn't get back to sleep with those two clowns clanging and banging around in the dark trying to fix what they'd broken so Boss would let them go hunting. It seemed as if he had just dozed off and gotten into the middle of one of his really good dreams, the one with the fourteen naked stewardesses and the midget surfer, when Cholly felt Boss poking him in the ribs and said loud and clear enough to wake the dead, "Hold on a minute, Sugar Baby. You're gonna be next."

"Get your gun, Cholly," Boss Bishop said, without saying so much as another word to anyone else but Jericho Walker, who was standing by the well watching the headlights on Mutt Binder's truck get dimmer and dimmer while Dan Steel and Mutt slopped around in the mud without fixing much of anything that Cholly could see, and one of them saying, "You ain't got to crap now, do you, Boss?" and Boss not even answering, just speaking low into Jericho Walker's ear and Jericho nodding.

Dianne was waiting in the truck. She was holding her scoped .257 Weatherby Magnum and Boss's iron-sighted

Sako 30-06 solidly between her knees, with the muzzles pointed toward the roof of the truck. Cholly laid June Bug down between them, muzzle to the floor, then got in.

"That gun unloaded?" Dianne Bishop asked as she scooted closer to the middle of the seat.

"Yes ma'am," Cholly Dormin told her and said he had once shot out the tire on a bird colonel's jeep with an unloaded rifle. "Somewhere in France," Cholly told them. "Maddest damn human being I ever saw. Said he'd have me court martialed if it wasn't the middle of a war."

"Cholly," Boss said. He was driving slowly down the sandy strip they called the Flag Pond Road, the truck's low beams shrouded in river fog. "How the hell could you shoot out a tire with an unloaded gun?"

Dianne shifted her legs, and now every time the truck hit a bump the rifles she was holding clicked together like antlers rattling.

"Anyway, I don't never load my gun till I get ready to hunt now," Cholly told them and said that was partly because June Bug's floor plate was about as reliable as a rubber crutch ever since he dropped her out of that scaly-barked hickory over by Jericho's Bridge last winter. Said June Bug liked nothing better than to spill her bullets out all over the ground the minute he pulled the trigger, so now he just used her like a single-shot.

"Cholly, do you just make all this up as you go along?" Dianne Bishop asked. They had turned around the edge of the small lake that was called the Flag Pond because of the deer's-tail resemblance of the pampas grass growing all around it. They were no longer on the road. Boss had switched off the lights and the truck was pitching back and forth like a small boat in a heavy sea.

"Did I ever tell y'all about the time me and Buzzard Wilson was fishing out in Mobile Bay and the motor quit?"

"Shut up, Cholly," Boss said, whispering now as he coasted to a stop. "Do *not* slam the door when you get out of the truck, Cholly. Do not talk. Don't even step on a dry leaf."

"I got to see a man about a dog," Cholly said.

"You just hold it, Cholly," Boss told him. "Jericho's been seeing a big deer looks like the great-great-grandson of Dianne's Bull. Says he's staked himself out a territory all the way from the Flag Pond to the Walnut Tree and over to the river." Boss got out of the truck and Dianne and Cholly got out the other side. Boss took his Sako from Dianne and then swapped rifles with Cholly. When he stuffed a wadded-up piece of paper into the top pocket of Cholly's shell vest, Cholly knew without looking that it was a hundred dollar bill. "For luck," Boss whispered.

It was cold that morning, too. Not quite thirty-five degrees, but the damp chill of the river made it seem worse than the dryer cold of other places. Daylight was only a gray promise in the southeastern sky and Dianne Bishop, who knew that big River Swamp and the woods around it as well as anyone alive, with the possible exception of her grandfather and Jericho Walker, knew they had less than half an hour to cover the mile of knee-deep sloughs and heavily wooded ridges that lay between them and the huge old black walnut tree that stood like a limbed fortress near where she had killed her Bull of the Woods so many years ago now it seemed as if someone else had done it.

They circled the Flag Pond and had barely walked two hundred paces into the woods when Boss indicated he was stopping. "One of you stop on the west end of Buck Ridge, and the other go on to the Walnut Tree," Boss said so lowly they could barely hear him.

By the time they got to Buck Ridge the sky had lightened enough for Dianne to see the features on Cholly Dormin's face. He looked so damned serious and strangely sad she almost felt sorry for him, but then he whispered, "You want me to miss him here, or walk on in to the Walnut Tree so we don't have so far not to drag him out?"

Dianne laughed. It was a low, very ladylike little giggle and she saw Cholly grin. "You take the Walnut Tree, Cholly," she told him. "But if you see that deer and don't put him on the ground, I think Granddaddy'll string you up from the game pole."

"Dianne," Cholly whispered, "if I was to do something that stupid I'd buy the rope and tie the noose myself."

The trouble was that Cholly Dormin did not actually know where the Walnut Tree was exactly, or at least he didn't know where it was in relation to where he was because he had only a very slim idea where he was right now. He had walked about a hundred yards in the direction Dianne had pointed him and then decided he had better relieve himself of some of last night's whiskey before he got to his stand, but when Cholly got through with his business he walked all the way to the river before realizing that not only was he not anywhere near where he was supposed to be, he was also completely out of the hunt.

It was getting very light so Cholly decided to go ahead and try to make the best of a bad and potentially embarrassing situation, him being somewhat of an expert at trying to make the best of bad and potentially embarrassing situations, and just stop and hunt as best he could from where he was. He loaded Boss's Sako with cartridges from his shell vest, worked the bolt to chamber a round, checked the safety, then sat himself down beneath the wide and spreading branches of a huge old live oak tree and went sound to sleep listening to water lap at the riverbank.

When they asked him later Cholly said he didn't think it was the shot that woke him up, but Boss's yelling and cussing sure did. He could tell it was coming from a long way off too and might even have been echoing over to the other side of the river and back, but Cholly said he knew as soon as he heard the volume of it that it had something to do with June Bug.

Cholly heard a commotion then and looked up just in time to see a big eight-point buck run past him and dive off the bank into the river. He had already eased the safety off the Sako and brought the gun up to his shoulder when he remembered Mutt Binders saying once that they'd sink if you shot them in the water, and then Boss saying that anybody who shoots a deer while it's trying to swim that river had best not be planning to ever hunt at Pineapple Bend again.

Cholly slipped the safety back on and laid Boss's walnut stocked Sako down in the soft dirt beneath the oak. He stood staring at the buck. It was already a third of the way across the quarter-mile-wide river and any stupid ideas Cholly might have been entertaining, that Cholly admitted later he actually did entertain momentarily and seriously, of somehow jumping on the buck's back and riding him over to the other side and then slitting his throat when the two of them came up out of the water together were quickly and best forgotten. Besides, Cholly had another plan.

He picked the Sako up, wiped most of the mud off the stock, then laid it across one of the low, thick limbs of the live oak for a rest. He was already trying to figure out exactly where the buck was going to come out on the opposite bank when Dianne Bishop walked up behind him and said, "You really don't make it all up, do you Cholly?"

"Put your scope on him and shoot him when he comes up out of the water," Cholly told her. "And don't never sneak up on a man like that again. You damn near made me wet my britches."

"You shoot him, Cholly," Dianne said, handing him her Weatherby and taking the Sako. "And I didn't sneak up on you. I've been watching you sleep for fifteen minutes."

Cholly Dormin got his deer that morning, too. He held the crosshairs of the scope Dianne Bishop had very carefully sighted in for two hundred yards squarely on the shoulder of the emerging buck and shot a great big hole in the middle of the river. He then proceeded to compound his felony by dropping Dianne Bishop's new Weatherby muzzle-first and scope to follow into the river mud there, so that when they heard a deer snort and turned around to see a nice three-point buck standing not thirty steps behind them and looking like he was hell bent and determined to get past them to the river, Cholly did not have the nerve to ask for the Sako back. Dianne handed it to him though, and that time Cholly didn't miss.

Back at the camphouse Mutt Binders and Dan Steel had just finished putting the toilet plumbing back together when Boss and Dianne and Cholly pulled into the yard with Cholly's buck.

"You all can crap now Boss," Dan Steel said. Boss just glared at him. Mutt Binders allowed as how Jericho and the rest of the hunters had gone back up toward Daisy Parker Hill, but didn't he hear three different rifles shoot somewhere between the Flag Pond and the river? Then Boss glared at him too.

"Cholly killed a deer," Dianne Bishop told the men who stood looking at the deer in the bed of her grandfather's truck.

"And it was a goddamned bona fide miracle, too," Boss grunted, then slammed the door of his truck so hard that Cholly's old gun fell off the fender Cholly had laid it on. Boss asked Cholly how much he wanted for June Bug. Said it was undoubtedly the sorriest excuse for a gun he had ever had the misfortune to shoot at a buck deer in his life, and that if Cholly would sell it to him he was going to have it cleaned up and give it to his worst enemy for a Christmas present.

Boss said not only did the floor plate fly open and dump bullets all over the ground the very minute he raised the rifle up to take aim at the biggest damn buck he'd seen in this swamp since 1952, said not only would the safety not go off until he figured out a way to hold the floor plate shut with his left hand while he pushed the safety off with his right thumb, said not only that but when he finally did get himself where he thought he could halfway shoot and the deer still had not had sense enough to run off, that when he finally did squeeze the trigger the hammer didn't fall right away but just kind of hung there vibrating for a second or two, not only did that sorry piece of Kraut ingenuity do all of that to him, but when it finally did take it upon itself to shoot the bullet fell two feet low and six feet left at fifty paces.

"The sights has been a mite out of line since I ran over her with the tractor," Cholly said, but Boss wasn't through yet. He said as soon as he got to town he was going over to City Hardware and order Cholly Dormin a brand new rifle with a scope on it, in the straightest shooting caliber Mr. Weatherby made, and that he was going to teach Cholly to shoot that gun like it was a part of him and teach him how to take care of the damn thing too, then dare him to let me ever see it with so much as a dirty fingerprint on it or even hear of him thinking about missing a deer with it either.

Cholly told Boss he didn't have to do that, but Boss said if he wanted to keep what little he had left of his sanity he did. "How much do you want for that piece of junk?" Boss asked Cholly then.

"Hundred dollars?"

"Sold," Boss said. He took two fifties from his money clip and handed them to Cholly, then grabbed June Bug and stomped off toward the kitchen, where they all heard him tell Queen Merry Walker to warm him up some breakfast before he lost what little bit of sanity he had left and her telling him, "Calm down now, Old Boss. You drink some of this coffee while I heats you up some of this ham and biscuits. Y'all ought to know better than go off without your breakfast. Puts you in a quander every time."

"I ain't seen Boss Bishop that mad since Blind Billy Benson shot that doe and tried to hide it under a pile of leaves," Mutt Binders said.

"Yeah," Dan Steel agreed. "What'd you do Cholly, shoot that deer out from under him?"

Dianne Bishop told them that all Cholly had done was get lost and then miss one deer and kill another, and that they didn't think either one of those deer was the deer her grandfather had missed. She said her grandfather always got like that when he missed a deer, but Cholly said it was about what he had expected all along. Told them his luck had gone from bad to worst ever since his mother-in-law broke her foot kicking his old dead dog Duck off the living room couch. Said he couldn't even go home now because he'd lost the rent money, not that he wasn't glad to know Queen Merry could get herself some teeth that fit now and she hadn't had a decent walking stick since she broke the one Boss gave her for Christmas over Jericho Walker's head, but he couldn't go home now because of it even with two hundred dollars in his pocket even if he wanted to because the first thing Dixie was going to do was notice June Bug missing, and then sure as hell Boss would do what he said, order that fine new gun, and Cholly said he knew he wouldn't have either the heart or the ambition to turn it down. Then his wife was going to think that not only was he sorry enough to gamble away the rent money, now she was going to think she had married the kind of man who wasted money on fancy new guns he couldn't barely afford.

"Well at least you got your deer today, Cholly," Dianne Bishop reminded him.

"Yeah," Cholly said with a big grin. "Ain't it funny how much better a man's luck gets when he really works at it?"

There was a silence then. Dianne looked at Cholly and shook her head. Mutt Binders cleared his throat and Dan Steel stared at the ground. Queen Merry Walker walked out of the kitchen holding June Bug by the butt and placed it in the trash barrel. "Old Boss says you come get yourself some breakfast, Dianne," Queen Merry said then. "And Mr. Cholly too can he keep his mouth shut long enough to eat."

Long Upon the Land

It was the last of the good hunts, when the land was truly theirs. Ross Dupriest never forgot being the first one there that night, nor the betrayal he felt because, in the end, he was the very last to know.

He had driven down from Tuscaloosa after classes that cool November Thursday and stopped by his parents' home in Garrison only long enough to load Maggy and Beau and a fifty-pound bag of the dry chunk dogfood the setters liked into the backseat of his old Volkswagen. He found some electrical tape in the garage and wound a piece tightly around the barrels and splinter forearm of the 16 gauge L.C. Smith his great-grandfather had bought new and four generations of Dupriests had shot the chokes out of literally but never taken time to repair the forearm which, for as long as Ross could remember, had tended to shoot loose at precisely the wrong time. He made himself a sandwich, changed into his hunting clothes, then left his parents a note telling them he would see them in the morning. He had turned off the blacktop and was less than two miles from the camphouse when he realized he had forgotten to bring any shells.

The night air was cold, and a damp breeze blew from the river. Ross let the dogs out of the car then stood watching them until his eyes adjusted to the darkness and he could see the outline of the stilted, wide-porched camphouse against the clear and starry sky. A light flashed through the trees, eerie and solid and so bright it hurt his eyes when he looked at it. Ross heard men shouting and soon he could see the running lights of a big tugboat and feel the deep throbbing of her engines as she struggled to keep her charge of coal-laden barges out in the middle of the river and away from the mud flats at the lower end of Pineapple Bend. He remembered how in summer if you were swimming in the river when tugs were churning past it would make a noise around your neck like a thousand snakes hissing, and you would remember all the stories of water skiers falling into balls of water moccasins, and even though you knew it was only the vibrations from the tug's propellers, it made you uncomfortable and wary until it stopped.

Ross climbed the thick, hand-hewn oak stairs and unlatched the screen door. He felt the old porch sag and creak as he walked across it, and without the starlight it was very dark. He ran his hand along the clay-chinked cypress logs until he came to the big, heavy door of the main room, and when he groped around inside until he found the bare bulb hanging in the center of the room and twisted the switch Ross was not surprised that nothing happened. He had a key to the box and knew how to turn the electricity on, but it had never mattered that much to him ever and tonight he was tired enough not to care at all. He struck a match and found a kerosene lantern sitting on the mantle above the big fireplace and turned the wick up and lit it. He let it burn brightly and black smoke poured form the wick while Ross wiped the globe clean. When he turned the wick back there was plenty of light.

Ross found the axe by the door and used it to cut a big piece of fat pine from the lighter stump Jericho Walker always left near the woodpile when he brought in a load of firewood. He put the kindling to his nose and smelled the fresh, clean, turpentine odor of the glycerin in the pine and thought of being sent out in the rain to cut a piece of lighter years ago and a thousand other times in between when they had come in from hunting or stopped because the dogs could not smell birds in the rain, and suddenly Ross Dupriest found himself very cold and badly in need of a fire. He laid his wood on the grate and held a match to the kindling until it caught, flickering yellow and then red in the dim, paneled room, and while the fire was growing Ross stacked armloads of extra wood outside the door and away from the screens, in case it rained. When the fire was going well he blew the lantern out and called the dogs in, then sat with them on an old sofa near the fire and listened to the noises the night wind made. When he was very sleepy Ross stretched out on the sofa with a tattered army blanket pulled over him. His dogs lay near him on another blanket he had thrown on the hardwood floor and as soon as they quieted down he went to sleep.

The dogs' barking woke Ross in the night and, because they never barked except at the shadows of a full moon or at a human being, Ross lay very still and listened. He heard a car door slam then recognized the voices of Forest Westbrock and his wife Charlene. Charlene was Ross's only aunt, her son Billy his only first cousin. He heard his aunt talking to her new husband in that familiar, syrupy, sorority house Southern drawl which Ross realized then, for the first time, was the way she really talked. I'll bet she's wearing makeup and jewelry in the morning, Ross thought, and looked at his watch. He could not make his eyes focus on the radium dial, so he told the dogs to hush then rolled over to go back to sleep. He thought how like Charlene it was to drive all the way up from New Orleans for the first quail hunt of the season and how like her it was to wake him in the middle of the night and neither apologize nor care. Ross had never disliked her though or forgotten that she had been the one who bought him his first gun and taught him to kill the quick gray mourning doves with the little .410 because if he could kill doves with that gun he could kill any bird with any gun, and she had been right. She had had the time to spend with him too, time that his father did not or could not find because in one town with one doctor there simply never was enough time ever. Beau lay with his head on his paws and growled lowly at the noisy couple settling into the next room. It's her perfume, Ross thought. It always screws up their noses.

"Burried down," Jericho Walker called in his deep, gravelly voice the next morning. The chestnut stallion and the saddle and the man and even his old, stained canvas coat were all so nearly the same dusty brown that only the man's thin lips seemed to move when he spoke. Maggy broke point to watch the faint chopping motion of the old man's hand, then, lifting her muddy paws very high and daintily, disappeared into the ash thicket where the first bobwhite quail had fallen.

"Four birds down?" Duncan Dupriest asked. He snapped open the breach of his Beretta Golden Snipe and let two spent 20 gauge shells fly over his right shoulder. Faint wisps of smoke evaporated into the crisp fall air.

"Burried down, Beau," Jericho Walker said. The big red and white setter turned to watch the second flick of the dark hand, then moved head-down and flag-high through the rows of gray, harvested soybeans toward the second bird. Jericho

Walker placed the bobwhite he had taken from the little lemon bitch into the canvas bag tied to his saddle horn then lifted his cap and scratched his wiry gray head as he turned to look down at Ross's father.

"Four birds down, Doctor," Jericho Walker said. "Come 'round Beau, come 'round. Put that nose down on the ground."

"I counted six shots, Jericho," Charlene Westbrock said. She stooped down to take a second bird from Maggy, and as she scratched the little dog's muzzle a gold bracelet slid from her wrist to the top of her thin buckskin shooting glove.

"Yes'm," Jericho Walker said.

"You didn't happen to see who missed, did you Jericho?" she asked. It was the question she always asked Jericho when someone missed, the question her grandfather had always asked him, even thirty-odd years ago when Charlene was a little girl and learning first to let the birds get up enough and not too much so they had too much speed or were too far away, and then to shoot at one bird and not all the birds and finally, when she was older and could handle a gun comfortably and well, to discipline herself not to see what Jericho called the "silly wets" of the bird's wings that her grandfather said were a false motion contrary to the movement of the bird, but to concentrate instead on the bird's head and to time her swing so that she fired at the bird's head and through it at the very moment her eyes focused on the bird's head, and since she had learned that Charlene Dupriest, now Westbrock, rarely missed.

"No'm," Jericho Walker answered, and told her the same thing he had always told her grandfather and, when Jericho was very young, he had said for the first time to Charlene's great-grandfather and made the old man laugh out loud. "Me and the dogs watches the burrieds. This hoss the only one looking at the guns, and he got sense enough to keep his mouth shut."

"I missed, Charlene," Ross Dupriest said. "And Frost pulled off when you stepped in front of him."

"She knows I wouldn't shoot her," Forest Westbrock said. He was Charlene's third husband and the only one of the three that Ross had liked at all. "I'd be much more subtle than that."

"Don't, Frost. Not even in a joke," his wife told him. "It's the worst sort of luck, and you know I didn't mean to block your shot."

"Sure, I know, Honey. Bad joke. Sorry."

"We should split up so we don't keep bumping into each other," Duncan Dupriest said. "Ross, you and Frost take Beau and hunt the windrow across Daisy Parker hill. Sis and I can hunt the edges around to the Possum Den well and wait for you there. Jericho, you ride over to the camphouse and tell Miz Dupriest to pick us up there around one o'clock, then go remind Queen Merry we need her to cook tonight and in the morning."

Jericho Walker nodded. He twitched the horse's reins with the same faint chopping motion he had used to control the dogs and rode slowly around the edge of the small field they had just hunted, becoming smaller and smaller as they watched the horse kick up huge gray clumps of the sticky fertile clay they called prairie mud.

"Old Jericho was born on this land, you know," Duncan Dupriest told his sister as they stood watching, waiting for Ross and Forest to get far enough away so they could resume hunting.

"Our father was too," Charlene reminded him.

"You're right. I forget that."

"It was the same year Queen's mother caught the kitchen on fire and burned the big house down. Don't you remember

Granddaddy telling us how they had to live in the hotel for over a year until the town house was finished and how bad he felt after he had built it because he could never afford to build anything but the camphouse on the land after that. Remember him telling us how he and Jericho cut cypress out of the Big Bottom and drug it up here with mules and chains? That's five miles through the River Swamp, Duncan. Just so he could build a camphouse by the river to sleep in when he hunted and fished."

"Sure, I remember, Charlene. What was it he used to say to us: 'First one misses has to do dishes'?"

"I haven't done dishes in twenty years, Darling," Charlene told him with a broad smile.

"Then don't miss, Darling," he said, and smiled back at her. He wondered if she knew how that perfume screwed up the dogs' noses. Probably, he thought. Handicapping herself so she won't get any easy shots, the way Granddaddy used to shoot pheasants lefthanded.

"Hunt Maggy, hunt. Hunt little girl," Charlene called as she flicked her hand toward the thick clumps of cocklebur and sedge near the edge of the field. Maggy began to quarter tightly through the harvested soybeans and into the grass, with Charlene and Duncan following closely behind. They jumped and scattered two coveys in less than half a mile, taking one bird each from the first and not letting Maggy hunt the singles and then, on the second covey, Charlene getting two going away right then left and very long on her second shot, and Duncan taking one that flushed straight back over his head when he stepped in front of Maggy, and blowing it to pieces and then with feathers raining down around him swinging quickly to take a fast-rising bird and missing cleanly with neither dignity nor grace.

"Nice bit of shooting, Darling," Charlene said, exaggerating her already exaggerated accent and grinning with catlike innocence.

Duncan grinned down at her. "Old Betsy seems to be patterning a bit unevenly," he told his sister. "Or perhaps it's these new shells."

"Of course," Charlene replied. It was their standing joke when either of them missed, begun when a very kind but addlepated Frenchman with a fine gun and no shooting eye whatsoever had lived for a year in the camphouse while helping their grandfather begin another of his regularly disastrous adventures in farming, this one a grape arbor, as if the Napoleonic exiles of the Vine and Olive Company had not been sufficiently defeated in their original attempt to do exactly the same thing their grandfather insisted he would not fail at but did. The Frenchman, they would soon learn, never missed but when his equipment somehow mysteriously failed him which was, of course, why the grapes all died that June.

"Want to swap guns for awhile?" Charlene asked. She loved outshooting someone with his own gun, especially Duncan because he had been the first of them to become a crack wingshot but never practiced now.

"The stock will be too short," he said, knowing exactly what she wanted to do.

"You know Frost wouldn't let me have the stock cut down on a trading gun," Charlene said.

"What is it?"

"A Parker, 28 gauge. See the engraving?" she said and held the receiver so he could see the silver spaniels and the big old pheasant in flight.

"What did he pay for it, Charlene? Five, six thousand?"

"Nearer thirty, I think. It's the condition and the gauge. And of course the engraving."

Duncan Dupriest broke the breach of his Beretta and laid it over his shoulder with the barrels pointing downward and back, then looked at his sister.

"What's the matter?" she said.

"I want to ask you something."

"Ask."

"Is Frost as well-off as he acts?"

"I don't like that question," Charlene said. "You know his family. You played basketball together in college."

"Not together. He's three years younger."

"Well he makes money on the guns, if that's what you mean. And we only shoot them if they've been shot before. It's not flaunting, Duncan. You should know that."

"I guess. It's just that you can never be sure. You know, the fine old families without a pot to pee in."

"We're an old family."

"That's what I mean."

"Is this about selling the land, Duncan?" she asked.

"We've had another offer, Charlene. The best one ever."

"The answer is no, Duncan. Period. Or have you forgotten we promised never to sell it?"

"That was a long time ago, Charlene. All the people we promised are dead."

"And that voids the promise?"

"Three million dollars, Charlene. That voids the promise."

"No," she said, then turned away.

"Don't you stand there with your goddamned thirty-thousand-dollar shotgun and turn your back on me, little sister. Do you know what a G.P. makes in a little two-horse town like Garrison? I couldn't buy two of your precious Parkers with what I netted last year. I could have worked three shifts a week at an emergency room in Mobile or New Orleans and done better. Ross starts medical school next year too, and that's one hell of an expense, especially since we barely get enough money from leasing the tillable acreage here to pay the taxes, Charlene. No ma'am. We are going to take this offer and nobody is going to stand in my way. Not you nor Billy nor your third rich husband either."

"Nor Ross?" Charlene asked. She turned to face her brother and stared at him with hard, blue eyes. "Have you told Ross yet? It was all supposed to be his and Billy's one day, you know. Don't sell this land out from under our children, Duncan, even if you don't give a damn about me."

"I already have, Charlene. Pop made me executor and I don't need your approval or anybody else's. It's over, done, and for one time in my life I don't have to worry about money or make stupid excuses about being 'land poor.' Don't you understand, Charlene? We're rich now. With real money, our own money. We can live where we want, do what we want whenever we want to do it. Be happy, Sis. Smile. You can't change it. Done is done."

Charlene Dupriest, now Westbrock, stood looking at her brother. She wondered what it could be that made a man who had never had to miss even one single meal in his whole life want money so badly he would sell the land four generations of his own flesh had traded their very lives for, and she did not know.

"Hunt Maggy, hunt!" she called, and when the little setter flushed a lone bobwhite quail Charlene tracked and fired and missed completely. She turned toward her brother then and stared at him. She did not blink, and when at last Duncan lowered his eyes Charlene threw the Parker in the dirt and walked away.

A Gentle Madness

Fall came late that year. It came with a long and gentle rain and the pungent odor of green wood burning. On the fourth morning the rain stopped, and the man and the woman drank wonderful strong coffee with fresh cream before going out to walk about their farm. It was cool, but they were young and close to summer so they left their shoes at the house. The mud felt smooth and slippery between their toes, and the new-fallen leaves the rain had loosed stuck to their bare feet. They sat on the bank of the river at the edge of their land, and spoke very little. There were giant water oaks there, never cut, and great, tall loblolly pines that together formed a cathedral of stately green spires and low, shadowy arches.

"Is it today?" she asked, her soft, gentle face resting on her knees.

"You know it is," he told her.

"But we've had so little time," she said.

"One year," he told her, though they had known each other all their lives.

"And fourteen days," she said.

"And fourteen days, and when I come back it will be like I never went away," he said and did not even believe it himself.

They walked together that afternoon, down the long, red-mud lane to the main road, and talked quietly while they waited. He kissed her when the bus came and held her tightly. She seemed so small and frail he thought that she might break.

"Come back to me," she said when he stepped up into the green, mud-splattered bus. He looked down at her and smiled, but his throat was so swollen with sadness he could not answer her and only waved. He sat in the back of the bus and watched her through the dirty glass, saw her standing there in the mud by the gate to their farm, waving to him and crying.

The driver of the bus was a very old man, but the rest of them were young men, going to war. They were singing and laughing and smoking, and each of them was scared. One had a brother missing in action and another had an uncle killed at Pearl Harbor. They were both very proud. When the bus had crossed the old wooden river bridge and started up into the hills the man could no longer see his wife and he began to relax. He could not sing with the others, but he took a cigarette the man with the missing brother offered him. He smoked it slowly as he watched the trees and farms and all of the country he had ever known pass by. He could not stop thinking of her, or wishing she would move into the town and not try to stay on in the leaky old house on the farm his grandparents had given them when they were married. It was their home and he knew she would not leave it, but with her parents dead and his so very old and most of the young men gone to war, there would be no one to help her. He thought of her often that day and each day of the three years he was away.

He stumbled through boot camp then crisscrossed the country on troop trains running on some secret, crazy wartime schedule of their own. At last he boarded a crowded troop ship that took him to England, where he stayed until they dumped him wet and scared in France. He walked and fought and crawled his way across Europe, all the way to the Rhine, and when he sat on the banks of that river and saw the bomb-blasted trees and the devastation of years of war that had torn the world like no other war ever, he had no thoughts but of his small and lovely wife with her soft red hair which looked black not red in the creased and folded photograph he carried in the liner of his helmet.

His company had mail call that day for the first time in many weeks, and there was no letter from her but one from her pastor. In a small, tight hand he had written:

"You will be pleased to learn that your wife is better now, though certainly not well. The women of the church are taking turns staying with her, as it will be some time yet before she will be able to care for herself." He took the letter with him back to the bank of the Rhine and sat there and read it and read it, but there was no more than that. He wept openly then for the first time since he was a very young boy.

When he came home it was summer and hot. She met him at the road and they stood together by their gate watching the cloud of red dust that followed the bus until they could not see it any more. They held each other tightly then for a long time, and nei-ther of them spoke until they turned to walk to the house. They held hands like children and walked with long, happy strides, but her eyes looked older to him and though she was only twenty-two there were streaks of gray in her lovely hair.

"It's awfully hot," she told him and sat beside him on the rough wooden steps. He held her then and kissed her. They sat for a long time in the bright heat of the day before either of them spoke.

"Are you okay?" he asked.

"Sure," she told him.

"I had a letter from your pastor a few months ago."

"Oh," she said, and looked away. "That wasn't anything."

"It scared me."

"A telegram came. It said you were missing."

"I didn't know."

"It upset me. That's all."

"Things got pretty confused there at the last. I got separated from my outfit for a few days. I'm sorry. I didn't know about the telegram."

"I'm all right now, honest. They sent a man to tell me you were okay. I just got upset."

"Let's walk down to the river," he said and began untying his shoes. "It's cool down there." He threw his coat and tie up onto the porch by his duffle, then they walked together barefoot to the riverbank. They undressed there, backs to each other, and swam in the cool, slow water of that river which, to him, was so unlike the Rhine. Later, when they were cool and pleasantly tired by the swimming, they lay together on the soft, thick moss beneath the spires and beams of their cathedral and made love quickly and with a great hunger for each other. They swam again then to cool themselves, then fell asleep in each other's arms.

When he woke she was lying beside him, playing with the thick black hair on his chest and watching his face. She seemed much as he remembered her, as if truly he had never left.

"I've missed you so," she told him when she saw that his eyes were open.

"I love you," he said, then pulled her close to him and kissed her. Thin, flickering sunlight played about them as this man and this woman, together now, loved each other slowly and easily and without haste or thoughts of any other time or place or thing. When it grew dark they dressed and walked back to the house, and when he lit the lantern on the mantle she began to talk and did not stop until after they had gone to bed.

He woke in the night and lay there, unable to sleep in the quiet stillness of the cool night. I won't have the dreams always, he thought, and after a time got up to build a fire in the iron stove in the kitchen and put a pot of coffee on to boil. He sat at the table and put some butter and the last of the strawberry jam on a piece of hard bread, and when he ate it, sitting there at their old, hand-me-down table, he felt as old and sad as a man can feel, and very far away. He did not hear her when she came into the kitchen, but he was not startled when she put her arms around his shoulders and touched her soft cheek to his. She poured coffee from the blue enamelled pot and apologized because there was no cream, then they sat and talked and told each other the things they wanted to tell, sparing each other the things that were too hard. When the sky began to lighten, became first gray and then a brilliant orange, he told her he would go fishing. She said she would come with him if he liked, but he said no, he would go alone.

He found the slough where he kept his boat, and after a while he found the boat sunk. The wood was waterlogged but not rotten, so he pulled the boat up into the sun to dry and walked down to the riverbank. He swam before he fished, to try to exorcise the sadness he had felt since waking in the night, and the swimming alone and later the fishing reminded him of the days and nights and countless summer hours he had spent there as a boy, and no one had to tell him then what was wrong. He knew that they both had changed, that the whole world had changed and that every man and woman and child left alive had lost something of great value none of them would ever regain.

By midday he had caught enough fish to feed them, and walking back to the house in the dusty heat made him think of marching tired and mind-dead on the dusty roads of France in summer and how such days in France had made him think of home. He passed quickly by the overgrown sadness of their fields, with ragweed and cockleburs growing where crops should have been. He felt badly then for having left her, though he had no choice, and wondered how she stood it there in springtime with no one to help her plant nor even a mule to pull the plow.

She fried the fish while he sat in the shade of the back porch and drank cool water from the well. She seemed happy to him then, and they did not talk until after they had eaten. She did not tell him how hard it had been, nor ever again speak of the time her pastor had written him, but as he sat there and watched her cook and hum to herself and smile, he thought he understood. When they had eaten she gave him the present she had bought him for welcome home. It was a new white shirt to replace the one that had yellowed in the drawer. It was the only new thing he had seen in the house, and when he opened it they held each other closely for a very long time.

Although it was already summer they used most of their money to buy a mule and seed, then plowed and planted side by side and remembered the late fall of the year he left, and prayed. They swam each evening in the river and made love on the soft, green bed of moss beneath their oaks and pines and slept well, as everyone who works hard must. The corn

they planted came up quickly and gave them hope, and by
mid-September it was taller than the man and well tasseled.
On the twenty-first he woke in the middle of the night to close
their bedroom window against the cold, and when he looked
out over their moonlit fields he saw a heavy, wet frost glisten-
ing on the cornstalks, and that was that. They had nothing in
the cellar and less than twenty dollars left of the money he
had saved from his army pay. When she woke in the morning
and saw the frost she turned to the mirror and began to brush
her hair. She did not cry out or even complain, but the man
saw the sadness again in her eyes and she seemed to move
more slowly through her days.

They ate fish and rabbit and venison throughout that fall
and winter and the few winter vegetables they could grow.
They got credit at the store too: not much, but they knew him
there and that he had fought in the war, though every day he
wondered why.

The spring came fast and with a big storm, and that night
their twins were born. The grizzled Creole midwife with sky-
blue eyes, granddaughter of slaves, who had birthed both the
man and his father before him, kept him from the room until
the worst of the storm had passed. When at last she let him
enter the old woman put her finger to her dry, cracked lips and
held him near the doorway with her eyes. His wife looked
pale in the dim light, and the babies the old woman held in her
arms slept and did not cry.

"No more," the dark woman told the man, and he understood.

His wife got stronger very slowly and did not have enough
milk for both their babies, so when he had broken the ground

for planting the man traded their mule for a cow and her calf. It pleased the woman to always have fresh milk for their boys and for coffee and to churn into good, rich butter, but she spoke very little now and her hair was as much gray as red. They made their crops by hand that year. She lay the babies near them on thick quilts in soft grass while they chopped and hoed and picked, but they did not visit their cathedral by the water's edge that summer nor any other summer again ever.

It seemed he only blinked and the twins were big boys going to school, fishing and swimming and hunting and running about the farm, adding something to their lives he had not even known was missing. She seemed better those years, he thought, when the boys were home and close. She liked doing things for them and their teasing, mischievous boyness. Those years were as a time suspended and set forever apart from the rest of their lives. They were all so wonderfully happy then it never seemed to matter that things were not really any better, for neither were they any worse.

He blinked twice and they were young men, bigger than he and handsome and strong. They looked and acted so much alike that they could fool him when they wanted to, but never their mother. They played football in high school and were both on the wrestling team, and neither of their parents ever missed a game or match. The boys were tough and good, with hard, young bodies, and the man and the woman were each very proud of both their sons. There were no scholarships though, nor money for college, and in the summer of their nineteenth years the army took them both.

It was very cold that winter and often rained for days without stopping. The woman spoke to him only in single words after the second boy left and spent her days always near windows that looked out toward the main road. She was the first to see the army car when it came, and there was blood in the screams the man heard as he ran crunching and stumbling across the icy stubble of his fields toward the house. A young captain was standing at the top of the steps when the man got there and told them both how very sorry he was.

The man held her while she cried there on the porch, then they walked together down to the river and found their old moss bed in the cathedral where the boy and his brother were conceived. She got down on her knees there, facing across the river, and gently pulled the man down beside her. Thin streams of tears ran down her face and fell onto her small bosom, and when she raised the tops of her fingers to her chin she looked so like a forlorn little child that he tried to embrace her, but she began to pray.

"Oh, Lord," she said in a choked, hoarse whisper. She did not close her eyes. "Bless our boy, bless his soul. Bless his soul and all the souls of all the boys lost in all the wars." She paused then, but when she seemed about to continue, to add some other thought, she closed her eyes and said "Amen."

"Amen," the man said softly, and they sat quietly together on the moss for a very long time. It was warm there, sheltered from the wind, and without either of them knowing when it started, nor how or why, the man and the woman made love in their cathedral by the river again and afterwards, when it was over, neither of them ever spoke of what they had done.

She hardly talked at all after that, nodding when spoken to and grunting when absolutely necessary. He took her to the doctor in town who said it was grief, which of course the man knew. The doctor tried to send her to a man in the city, but she would not go, then when spring came and they were busy with the planting she seemed a little better. Their other boy came home that summer and she was more herself for awhile, especially at first. There seemed to be something missing in him, though the woman noticed it more than the man. It was as if the boy were smarter and tougher yet somehow less than he was before, and he seemed always to have a chip on his shoulder. He hurt a man in a fight that winter, hurt him badly. It was not the first time but it was the worst and they put him in prison for it. The woman never visited him there and the man did only once. When the boy saw his father waiting behind the black steel grate he turned and disappeared back into the bowels of the prison.

The boy came home when he got out. He was bigger and stronger and so much older they hardly knew him. He had a cast in one eye and could barely see out of it, but he would not tell them how it happened. The woman seemed better with him home and that pleased the man, but the boy came in drunk the third night he was there and cursed his mother then slapped her, not hard but across the mouth. When the man came running into the room and saw the red blood trickling from her small, soft lips he knew exactly what had happened. He knocked the boy to the floor and kicked him as he lay there not fighting back, stomped him and would have hurt him badly had not the woman grabbed the man and screamed for him to stop. The man sent their son away that night and they have heard nothing from him since.

Her hair is gray now and they both are old. She sits on the front porch each day and rocks and watches, and at night she leaves a light on in the parlor. In her restless sleep she calls out for both her boys and often wakes the man. He holds her then and tries to calm her, but her sleep is deep and she does not wake.

The woman cannot tell him what she dreams of now, but he pretends to know. She dreams of the good times when they were young and close to summer and of the boys when they were truly theirs. She dreams of their cathedral by the river too, and of a world where there is no war. Those are the dreams the man hopes she has, that he prays for her to have. For hers is such a gentle madness.

Fathers

When Dianne Bishop was twelve years old her parents died. This did not leave her destitute, there was insurance and her grandfather was a wealthy man, nor unwanted, the Dupriests would have been glad to take her in if Boss Bishop had not. But it did leave her, in a way she thought no one else would ever understand, alone.

"Does God laugh at us?" she asked that night after the crowd of mourners had gone and the house was very quiet. Her grandfather was downstairs and his cook and house-keeper, Queen Merry Walker, was putting Dianne to bed.

"No, child," Queen Merry Walker said. "God don't laugh at folks." She flapped a quilt out over the bed, sending the smell of musty air circling around the room. The quilt and the bed and the bedroom and everything in it had once belonged to Dianne Bishop's father. Dianne sneezed.

"Scat, Haint," Queen Merry said. She meant it like Gesund-heit, a blessing.

"Queen," Dianne Bishop said. She was under the covers now, with only her small face and dark hair showing in the high old bed. Queen Merry was having to prop the window open with a stick because, as old as the house was, its foundation was still settling. When it was laid in the summer of 1851 a slave named Isaac True and said to be an ancestor of Queen Merry Walker was killed setting a piling. It was a story Queen Merry had told Dianne many versions of, all of them sad and all of them ending with Queen Merry's assertion that Isaac True was the reason the house's windows and doors would not open or close properly. "Settling on his bones," Queen Merry would say.

"Queen," Dianne said again. Queen Merry was humming to herself a song which sounded very much like "Amazing Grace."

"Yes, child," Queen Merry Walker said. Queen Merry called every young person, black or white or the son of the Chinese missionary who once visited the congregation of the Saint James African Methodist Episcopal Church "child." Adults were "Misters" or "Missuses," depending, and those not in favor she prefaced with "that."

"Did you ever see anybody die, Queen?" Dianne Bishop asked.

"Hush, child," Queen Merry said. "Folks don't supposed to talk like that."

"But didn't you ever?" Dianne said. She had been told only that her parents had been killed in a train wreck. The newspaper, which she had read secretly and with morbid fascination, told her that Mr. and Mrs. Jack (Edie, nee Edie Perril of Tuscaloosa) Bishop, only son and daughter-in-law of Garrison businessman Granville C. (Boss) Bishop, had been killed along with seventeen other passengers and two crewmen when the City of New Orleans plunged tragically into the shallow waters of Lake Pontchartrain. The couple had been visiting with friends in the Crescent City during the recent Mardi Gras festivities. Donations to a favorite charity, and that was all.

Queen Merry sat down. She was a big woman, tall and with the wide, square shoulders of a man. The old chair creaked as she rocked in it. "What you wanting to know, child?" Queen Merry asked. "You wanting to know did Queen ever see somebody dead, the answer is yes'm. Too many. Time you're my age you'll of seen too many, too. But you say did I ever see somebody die, the answer is yes'm too, 'cause I seen that too."

"Who, Queen?" Dianne asked. She was sitting up in the bed with her legs drawn up to her chest and her arms around her legs. She was conscious of her own breasts now, new and small, and the sound of the rocker creaking. The floor lamp behind Queen Merry was very dim and its light shown soft and yellow on the sloped, papered ceiling.

Jack and Edie Bishop had lived in this room when they were first married, stayed there on and off for the three and a half years it had taken Jack to settle down and take a job at his father's bank. Edie said it was a cozy room, like the attic rooms you found in old Swiss inns. Dianne, who had never been to Switzerland in her life but was convinced she had been conceived there, agreed.

"My daddy," Queen Merry said. "Only I was littler than you, and I can't tell it so good. Don't much like telling it no-way."

"Was he killed?" Dianne asked. She was learning the semantics of death. How death came and how people felt about it were very important to her now.

"No'm," Queen Merry said. "He just die. We was hoeing peas and he say 'Queen go fetch me some water,' and when I did he took a sup and then rolled his eyeballs back and die."

"I'm sorry, Queen," Dianne Bishop said, and she truly was, hearing something she must have heard before but only now understood.

"It was hot," Queen Merry said. "It was hot blaziner than hell fire and him with his old bald head and done lost his hat somewhere and couldn't find it or buy no other one neither till the crops made. So he say. Only your granddaddy'd a give him one if he'd a asked. Mama said that. Man dead on account of his pride and what he got to show for it. Die young too. That's what Mama said. Over and over. Die so young and what for?"

"I'm sorry, Queen. I didn't know."

"Jesus come though. I seen that," Queen Merry said. "Papa laying there dead on the ground and the clouds come up and the wind come up thrashing across the tops of that big stand of willow trees and then raking down across them peas like a line of rain coming, only there wasn't no rain. It was Jesus. That's what Mama say too. 'Here come Jesus get this fool.' "

Then Queen Merry Walker stopped talking. Dianne could almost physically hear the sound of an old, thick door being closed between them, a door she had only begun to know was open. It had never been open before. She watched Queen Merry rocking, saying nothing; nothing was in her eyes. It seemed like a very long time before Dianne finally spoke. "Where's Granddaddy?" she said then.

For a moment Queen Merry did not answer. When she did she spoke quietly, not in her own voice, or in a voice she had not used in a very long time. "I speck he downstairs drinking whiskey and grieving," she said. "Folks do that. You done lost a mama and daddy but Old Boss done lost a son. Don't know which is harder. Don't never want to find out which is harder neither. No'm."

"You mean True," Dianne Bishop asked. Queen Merry Walker had a son Dianne's age, her only child. His name was

Harry S. Truman Walker. Harry S. Truman was elected Vice President of the United States of America in 1944, the year both Dianne Bishop and Queen Merry's son were born. Queen Merry told people she had heard that Harry Truman stood up to the Ku Klux Klan, and she wanted her son to grow up being that kind of brave. But nobody ever called him Harry, not even Queen. They called him True.

When Dianne Bishop's grandfather came to check on her it was late, after midnight she thought, though she wasn't sure. Dianne had no watch and the courthouse clock had developed a worn sear which caused the hammer to slip a notch at midnight and strike thirteen times. Replacing the hundred-year-old sear had proved impractical and the chimes were silenced forever. Better not to know what time it was than have a clock strike thirteen times.

"Are you awake, Dianne?" her grandfather said, but she did not answer. He smelled of whiskey and cigar smoke, and when he sat on the edge of her bed near the open window Dianne heard the old man sigh so deeply his throat rattled. That must be what it sounds like when your heart breaks, Dianne Bishop thought. She had heard the same sound in her own throat earlier, at the moment the pallbearers slid the two matching caskets simultaneously into the two matching graves and Dianne understood for the first time what forever means.

"Your daddy was a happy man," her grandfather said. He had pushed the edge of the screen back to he could flip the ashes from his cigar out the window. Still Dianne feigned sleep, though she wanted to talk. She had never before thought of her mother or her father as people who were happy or unhappy or even good or bad. They were simply her parents, and other than feeling that nebulous attached acceptance people called love, Dianne realized now, she had hardly known them at all.

"They used to call this place Bishop's Ferry," her grandfather said. "Did you know that?"

"Yes," Dianne Bishop said. It did not seem to surprise her grandfather that she was awake.

"You know why?" he asked.

"For Old Granville?"

"That's right," he told her. "For Old Granville. He was granddaddy to me like I'm granddaddy to you."

"I know," Dianne Bishop said.

"Never met the man," her grandfather told her.

"He was killed in the Civil War, wasn't he?" she asked. Dianne was lying with her elbow on the bed now, her face in her open palm. She could feel the weight of her grandfather near her, saw his silhouette in the moonlight, the red glow of his cigar.

"Yes and no," her grandfather said. "The War Between the States was over, more than a year. You know why this town's called Garrison now?"

"My teacher told us it was named after some famous abolitionist."

"Ha!" her grandfather said, "not hardly," then told her how his own grandfather, defeated in war and left with very little money, with only his land and family still to call his own, had come home to find a company of Yankee soldiers garrisoned in his house, using it as headquarters for the guard that was still in charge of the ferry.

"This house," her grandfather said, and there was a tone in his voice Dianne had not heard before, an indignation seeming neither hot nor new: heat without fire. "In this very house," he said. "But not in this room. We built this room after Jack was born."

"And that's why they call it Garrison now?" Dianne Bishop asked. "Because those soldiers were garrisoned here?"

"In part," her grandfather said and told her how his own grandfather had come home, through with fighting and war and all manner of disagreement mankind has made himself susceptible to, ready at last to find peace again in his own life and in his own spirit; a strong man not broken but weakened forever by what he had done and seen and knew even then he might still have to do, had come home to find not peace, but that what would prove to be the worst was just beginning. Old Granville Bishop, who was forty-six years old when the War Between the States was ended and the South surrendered and he came home, would not for over a year yet regain the broken hollow shell which once had been his home, her grandfather told her. He would live instead in the middle of his own land, in the place men called the Big Bottom even then, in a house he built himself of canvas and wood, hunting and fishing to survive while his fields lay not only fallow but sprouted trees and brush that would take time measured in years to clear. He would bury his wife before six months was out, dead of cholera at the old age of forty-five; their son and daughter still children.

"He wasn't back in this house a week when he dropped dead," Dianne Bishop's grandfather told her. "Probably had a stroke."

"Like Queen's daddy," Dianne said.

"Queen's daddy gave himself a sunstroke," her grandfather said. "But I guess it's about the same. I guess when you get right down to it, we all kill ourselves one way or another."

"Mama and Daddy didn't," Dianne Bishop said. She thought she had missed something or that this was one of those things she was not supposed to be old enough to understand.

"Some folks would argue that," her grandfather said. "You get on a train you don't have to be on and it wrecks, or even just go outside and get struck by lightning when you could have stayed in the house. But I don't believe that. It's just that living itself seems to use up whatever it is that living is, and there's not very much we can do about that."

"Oh," Dianne Bishop said. "But why Garrison?"

"Not to forget," her grandfather said and told her he didn't guess there was any way for men like Old Granville Bishop to ever forget, but it was wrong to want and try to make the next generation and even the next and the next hold onto a grudge for you until nobody living had anything left but the grudge, no matter how well-founded that grudge was. Said his own grandfather had put it in his will that under no circumstances whatsoever was the name Bishop to be used in connection with any business or place name within the area once known as Bishop's Ferry.

"Haven't you noticed our name's not on anything around here?" her grandfather asked, then said, "Technically I could lose this house and all the land around Pineapple Bend by so much as putting my own name on the front gate. You remember that, time comes it's yours. Those little ladies down at the Hysterical Society would like nothing better than to get their hands on Granville Bishop's house. You could beat them, it's an old will, but you can bet your eye teeth they'd try to have it declared a historical site and sell tickets. Never saw anybody so damn interested in somebody else's past."

"He must have hated them," Dianne said. "The soldiers."

"Hate's not half strong enough a word for what Old Granville must have felt by the time he died, Dianne. I don't think they've got a word for that kind of bitter."

"I think Queen's bitter like that," Dianne Bishop said, surprising even herself. "About her daddy, and the way she calls True after that Isaac True that died over a hundred years ago."

"I know she is," her grandfather said. "But Queen's bitter is different, too. She doesn't have any hope for herself. She hasn't given up, never will. No more than Old Granville did or would have if he'd lived. But Queen's got no money or power, either, and her and Jericho are both smart enough to know that without one or the other there's not much hope for their generation.

"Hell, Dianne," her grandfather said. "Queen's ignorant. She probably doesn't even know what words like next generation and inherited guilt and bequeathed hatred or whatever you want to call it mean. But she's not stupid. Don't ever think ignorant and stupid mean the same thing. They don't.

"Her and Jericho both know what they want. They've got that boy True, and sure as the world they're putting every bit of faith and hope they've got into him, laying it all on the next generation and hoping for the next and the next, just like Old Granville did ninety years ago.

"But the trouble is, the hate's going to come through. Queen feels it. She'd never admit it to you or me in ten thousand years, but she feels it. I feel it myself and you and True will one day too, if you don't already. Might all of us up and explode one day. This whole South."

"But Garrison," Dianne Bishop said. "That's so awful. Did he name it that?"

"He did," her grandfather said and told her there weren't that many people living here then, and that those who did had not only had a rough time with the war itself but a rough time on a very personal level because of the garrison stationed here. The fact there was a Yankee abolitionist by the name of William Lloyd Garrison was a perverse joke only those who had lived through the trouble could appreciate.

"A joke?" Dianne said.

"Kissing the Devil," her grandfather said, then "People laugh hardest at what scares them the most."

"Oh," she said. They were quiet for a while then. There seemed to be nothing more to say. Boss Bishop pushed out the edge of the screen and tossed his cigar into the night. Dianne pulled the covers up around her, suddenly cool. She thought of her parents, their love of travel. In their thirteen years of marriage Jack and Edie Bishop had been to Europe half a dozen times, to Canada, Alaska, Mexico, South America, to Africa hunting twice and they had already booked a third safari for the coming summer. This time they were going to take Dianne. She was old enough now, her parents had said.

"Didn't you ever want to just leave this place, Grand-daddy?" Dianne asked then.

"Leave Garrison?" he said, then "Once. No, more than once. But I only really left one time. Me and Doc Dupriest."

"Doctor Duncan?"

"Mm-hmm. Doc Ross wasn't even born yet. In fact, Doc wasn't even a doctor, still in college. I was running a timber crew for my pa. About twenty, both of us. That would have been 1908 or '09. Decided we'd try our luck at sea. Doc, we called him Dunc then, had been studying *Moby Dick* in some English class and he made me read it because he figured that since our granddaddy..."

"He was Doctor Duncan's granddaddy too," Dianne Bishop said. She knew that but had forgotten it. Family history confused her.

"That's right," her grandfather said. "Little Charlene Dupriest has as much of Old Granville in her as you do."

"I hadn't thought of that," Dianne said. Charlene Dupriest, two years younger, was someone Dianne thought of more as a playmate than a relative, seeing her at church and school and occasionally when they both went hunting with their grandfathers.

"So since Old Granville was supposed to have first come to this country as an able-bodied seaman and jumped ship at New Orleans, me and Dunc decided we ought to see if we didn't have some salt in our blood too," her grandfather said and told her how the two of them had slipped out of town on the milk train, rode it north to Tuscaloosa, and hopped a through freight to New Orleans. There, for not much more than passage and meals, they shipped out on a freighter bound for the Middle East with a load of sugar. They jumped ship in Alexandria, Egypt, no saltier than their ancestor.

"Ducks that should have stayed out of water," her grandfather said. "Miserable. Took us two months to get back to Garrison. Never been so happy to see a place in my life."

"But what about the hate?" Dianne Bishop said. "Isn't that what you were trying to get away from? Wasn't it still here when you got back? Weren't you still who you were?"

"Dianne," her grandfather said. "I don't think you can run far enough or fast enough to get away from who you are. And the worst kind of lonely I ever knew was being somewhere I didn't belong trying to be somebody I wasn't. Miserable."

"Granddaddy," Dianne Bishop said. He looked at her but did not speak. "Do you think God laughs at us?"

"Ha!" her grandfather said. He stood up and walked to the foot of the bed. Dianne could see his face in the moonlight. He looked very old to her.

"Ha!" he said again.

"I asked Queen," Dianne told him. "She said He doesn't. But I don't know. It's like this is all some bad joke that I don't understand. It's like I'm not even meant to understand."

"Ha!" her grandfather said. "Queen would say that. Queen never had people working for her, never watched people whose livelihoods you're responsible for get themselves into the same stupid messes over and over again and wait every time until it's too late before they ask you to help them straighten it out.

"Hell," her grandfather said. "Last year when old man Bob McMillan cut his little finger off on the ripsaw, I helped him get the insurance company to pay him a thousand dollars for it. Must have impressed hell out of that McMillan bunch, too, because last week old Bob's boy come to work for me and first thing he did was cut two fingers off on the same saw, only it was on his left hand and he would have had to been standing on his head for it to be an accident.

"Come to the office with them two fingers wrapped up real neat in a little rag and asked me when did I reckon he could get his two thousand dollars. Said he was getting married in a week and needed the money to buy himself a new car."

"That's awful," Dianne Bishop said.

"It's awful because it's true. Poor damn fool. But I didn't laugh at him, Dianne. I didn't even fire him. Hell, wouldn't nobody else ever give him a job after what he'd done."

"You didn't do anything?" Dianne asked. "After he did something like that?"

"Fired his daddy," her grandfather told her. "Figured it was mostly his fault anyhow, and one of them had to go. Ain't no business big enough to work two fools. You remember that. And quit worrying so much about what God's doing. Let Him worry about that."

"I don't think He laughs at us, though," Dianne Bishop said. "Do you?"

"No, Honey," her grandfather told her. "I don't think He laughs at people, not even fools. And we're all fools in one way or another."

"I'm glad," she said then. "I'm glad you think that and Queen thinks that. Life wouldn't make sense if it's all just a big joke."

Or unless it is, her grandfather thought then, though he did not say it. His granddaughter was still a young girl and who knows, maybe she would be the one Bishop to finally figure out what they were there for, and why the hell they couldn't seem to leave.

The House at Blue Mountain Beach

It was raining hard now, and very cold. A man named Robert Gardner stood in the dim shelter of the house's low porch, watching the storm and the sea. The wind was blowing hard straight in from the Gulf of Mexico the way he remembered it would sometimes do, stinging his face and rushing the waves in fast so they slammed into each other and sprayed skyward a dozen feet or more then hung there, frozen, seeming for long moments to glow with a pale green light that must have come from the white sand of the ocean floor and not the gray November sky, then dropping suddenly downward onto the beach and hitting it continually with the dull, thudding sound of human hands beating furiously upon the loosed drumheads of a thousand giant tympani. Standing there, shivering with wet and cold but enraptured still by the light and the foam and the sound of the drumless drummers' muffled beatless beatings; come now at last to ponder and sort and try to make sense of the flotsam and jetsam that was all that remained of the shipwreck of his life, it seemed to Robert Gardner that it must have been raining for a very long time.

It was his house now, had been for more than twenty years, but for more than twenty years now he had rented it to others in season while out of season paying other others to see to its upkeep, so that the house had remained the same while everything around it was changing. Coming in on the beach road that afternoon he had driven past one condominium after another, each rising up from the rolling white dunes with unnatural unwelcome alacrity to remind him of giant bleached mausoleums, and Robert Gardner was very pleased to find that so far none had been built near the house at Blue Mountain Beach.

It was painted a deep blue now, faded-looking even in the rain but not the light gray it had been that last November he had seen it, the way he always thought of it and even dreamed of it, because no matter what else that last fall and the summer before it had been, it had also been the last free and truly good season of Robert Gardner's life. And as if to remain the single unchanging constant standing alone to anchor his life of multiple erratic uncertainties, betrayals and disappointments, the house stood now in loyal sameness despite its dark color, low and solidly small and not quite stately, with its long gabled roof swept back away from the edge of the low white bluff that was called Blue Mountain, so that from the beach you could not see the house itself but only the very crest of the roof and the tops of the two big river-rock chimneys. Robert Gardner knew too that you could only see the whole house from far out in the Gulf and always remembered that the first time he had seen it that way he had been out on his grandfather's boat and refused to believe that the small gray box the others were pointing to was the house his grandfather had built, until the old man had let him climb up onto the tuna tower where he had never been allowed before, to look through the big heavy glasses that his grandfather used to spot birds working the schools of fish. Robert had seen not only the whole house then but saw his mother too, sitting on the porch where he was standing now, wearing a new and brightly colored sun dress, reading her morning papers and drinking her coffee, looking so pretty and close to him then through the glasses that the boy had waved and called to her, and he remembered feeling bad for a very long time because she had looked toward him but never waved back.

There had been a young woman too, that last good summer and fall, and some bad things. Robert Kennedy had died. Robert Gardner remembered that with absolute clarity because he lost his college deferment the same day, and talking about it at dinner that night his father had said that three bad things always happened together and reminded Robert that the sixth of June was also the twenty-fourth anniversary of the day Eisenhower had dumped him and all the other Great Last Hopes of the Free World onto the beaches at Normandy.

"Were you scared?" Robert Gardner had asked his father then.

"No," his father had told him; this great man, his father, whom Robert Gardner could not then imagine ever being afraid or even scared; this man who had fought bravely in France and been so terribly wounded in Germany that he had almost died, and still slept badly every night because the tiny bits of shrapnel around his spine could never be removed; this man who had thought after the war that he could join his own father's law firm for just long enough to put some money aside to live on and then quit to write a book about the war, who had even published two stories about the war that to Robert Gardner, reading them later, had seemed better than the stories of Mailer or Hemingway or James Jones, or anyone else who was writing then about soldiers and war. This was the man who told Robert Gardner that he had not been scared on Omaha Beach but added, thoughtfully, "Not then, Bobby. I was past scared then. Words like scared and afraid are for when you've still got a choice between fighting and running, and there on that beach there wasn't anything left to do but fight or die, or maybe fight and die, but either way that's not any choice at all."

"But can't a man who won't fight be a brave man too?" Robert Gardner would always remember asking that night.

"No," his father had told him, looking very serious now. "Not in our time. Maybe not ever."

Two weeks later Robert and his mother had gone to the house at Blue Mountain Beach for the summer while his father stayed in Atlanta to work on the unusually heavy case load he had carried for the law firm of Gardner, Simmons, and Plott since the death of Robert's grandfather the year before; this when Robert knew that surely his father was wealthy enough by now to give up at least part of his case load and begin writing the book that Robert Gardner continued to believe his father would write until the day his father closed the door to his office, lit a cigarette and placed it in the otherwise spotless ashtray, then took the big army forty-five he kept in his desk drawer and put a single, not quite half-inch hole through the center of his heart.

He left one note, addressed to Robert, unsigned. It said, simply, "Never stay too long, Son."

There was a short sad funeral at the Buckhead house, attended and nearly overwhelmed by men in pin-striped suits and women who smelled like the vodka they thought did not smell, uttering simple somber condolences they probably meant, so that Robert was glad when his mother told him to go back to Blue Mountain Beach and close up the house. She would sell it, she had told him as he was leaving, and Robert did not argue, but his father had robbed in death that great lady of fine gestures the flurry of fine and final gestures he had known she would make, ridding herself of all that remained of his life as she had sold her own father's house and car and even given his horses and perfectly matched pair of springer spaniels, that almost no one could tell apart when they were working birds, to a farm for needy children; Robert's father forestalled her completely and forever by leaving his money and all his possessions to his son and leaving his wife to subsist on that very small fortune her father had left her and which she would never share with Robert's father, not even long enough for him to write his book. A fine poetic justice that, Robert Gardner thought as he settled into the house at Blue Mountain Beach then, his house now, to await the inevitable draft notice or the coming of fall, not much caring which befell him first.

He met Dianne Bishop in August, met her and came to love her quickly with a depth that frightened him. By early September he had asked her to move into the house at Blue Mountain Beach and they stayed there, together, on through October and into November, so that on the morning when they at last crossed the border into Canada it was bitterly cold and snowing and the FBI had already been to the Buckhead house, had talked to Robert's mother, shamed her in front of her friends as the government pursued its unrelenting search for yet another young man who had refused to ask not what his

country was doing in Vietnam or even to keep his Appoint-
ment in Samarra; shamed her thoroughly she told him, though
he knew there must have been some motherly decency and
concern or maybe even what passed with her for love left within her bitterness, because she had called him that night, if only
to tell her only son that she would not lie for him again.

Dianne Bishop had not stayed. She loved him he knew but left
him anyway so that again he felt as if a very bad thing had happened to him for no reason, packed her one small leather suitcase
during the middle of their third cold Calgary winter and left him
without even telling him she was leaving or why. And as old as
that old memory was Robert Gardner still hated it, hated it worse
even than the much more recent memory of the wife of fourteen
years who had left him this past September, because there the love
had gone before the leaving, and even Robert Gardner had been
surprised to learn how easy leaving was when love had gone.

She had seemed like such a strange woman at first, Dianne
Bishop had, somehow very different from the girls he had
known and older too, woman not girl, and though at twenty-
four she was only three years older than Robert Gardner, no one
would ever call Dianne Bishop a girl again. She was an artist,
an artist who lived then in a small rented house less than a mile
down the beach, a painter of seascapes and birds who sold what
she could to the tourist shops in Panama City and Fort Walton
and Pensacola, or sometimes when things were slow packed the
trunk of her old beige Chevrolet with her small canvasses in
their bright varying watercolor shades of blue and red and yellow and white, the only colors she ever used, and drove to New
Orleans to hawk her paintings in Jackson Square.

Robert had gone with her once, to New Orleans. Dianne
had sold a dozen paintings by noon, but instead of partying

away the rest of the day and night in the French Quarter, as Dianne had assumed they would do, Robert instead drove them down to his grandfather's old duck lease in Plaquemines Parish.

Emile Broussard, the old Cajun who owned the land there, remembered Robert Gardner, though he seemed to think that Robert was actually Robert's father, and for a hundred dollars cash let Robert use a somewhat less than seaworthy old pirogue and a dilapidated but guaranteed accurate Winchester pump, threw in a half box of shells and pointed Robert and Dianne toward Robert's grandfather's favorite spot in the marsh.

Robert killed two ducks that afternoon, both mallards, which, considering he had no decoys and only his own mouth and a wide piece of sawgrass for a call, Robert thought was a blessing. But what inscribed the hunt so indelibly on his mind was the way Dianne Bishop had sat so quietly in the front of the small, shallow boat with her sketch pad braced on her knees, drawing furiously the whole time they were there, oblivious to Robert and barely even noticing the two times he shot. A week later she gave Robert two watercolors, one for each duck she told him, and in them she had captured the austere, lonely beauty of the marsh in autumn, of ducks flying low across blue skies dotted with shattered white clouds and the coldness of the last orange glow of the setting sun, all in a way that made him truly believe Dianne had somehow discovered the essence of a beauty he had stumbled blindly through the midst of all his life.

She told Robert once, after the last trip she had made to New Orleans before she moved in with him, that an art dealer there had bought seven of her watercolors and had told her that her work showed a great deal of raw talent and energy but lacked discipline entirely. Robert was surprised how much that had pleased her. He knew nothing of artists then but had often heard his father speak of the intense discipline necessary to prepare for an important trial and how he would someday turn that same discipline to his writing and use it to quickly surpass the sloppy young hacks who were writing bestsellers now. Then Robert's mother would say, "But oh, you would have to write us a bestseller every year to make what you make with the firm," and the conversation about writing would be over for that day.

Robert soon learned that, unlike his father and despite her undeniable ability, Dianne was slave to a lack of discipline she mistook for independence. Truly she was more impatient than independent, he could see that. Temperamental too, and lazy, though in her the laziness was never sloth but the laziness of a beautiful spoiled cat, luxurious and haughty and not to be disturbed, and he loved her for it. She seemed always to have money, yet to own nothing but her clothes and the old car and a great deal of heavy gold jewelry, though nothing with any stones, and she invariably wore some of the gold around her wrists and her throat and in her small, flat, pierced ears, so that when she pulled her dark hair back behind her wide, tan face and tied it with one of the brightly colored scarves she always wore, Dianne Bishop seemed more beautiful than simply pretty to Robert Gardner, despite the little-bit too thick dancer's legs she worried so much about.

A strange, beautiful woman. That's what Robert Gardner had said yesterday when he made the mistake of stopping to see his mother and the man who was technically his stepfather now at the Buckhead house, which was technically Robert

Gardner's house, and then made the second mistake of telling his mother about his divorce and the third mistake of talking about Dianne Bishop, whom his mother had met once and formed her own opinion about. Robert knew he had been adamantly stupid yesterday, trying to explain the idiosyncrasies he had cherished in Dianne Bishop: the way she was always ready to act on her impulses and never bitched about the consequences and how she seemed so honestly, blessedly free and quite incapable of any emotion or feeling that could even remotely be called guilt or fear or remorse.

That was when he saw that his mother's eyes had clouded over with that cold dense wall of hatred she had once reserved for his father, that opaque wall beyond which she had never admitted anyone nor tried to reach out beyond herself to understand anyone, not even her husband, not even her son, not tried to nor even cared to try. Robert Gardner stopped talking then. He clamped his jaw shut as he went to his father's old study to get what he had come home to get, but paused when he saw that that room was the one thing in the house his mother had not dared to change. The pictures on the wall, black and whites mostly, were the same pictures Robert remembered from the first time he had been old enough, thirteen or fourteen he thought, to be allowed into the dark and manly depths of his father's sanctum sanctorum, his one inviolable retreat.

Pictures of Robert's father and grandfather hung there, of the two of them together with dogs and guns and birds and boats and fish, both of them always smiling. On one there was a shiny new pre-World War Two Cadillac with a teenager barely recognizable as Robert's father behind the wheel and Robert's grandfather standing in front of the car with one foot

up on the bumper and his arm around a very young looking
Emile Broussard. The hood of the Cadillac was covered with
ducks, thirty or forty Robert guessed, and knowing what stick-
lers his father and grandfather had been for obeying both the
letter and spirit of the law made him think there must have
been no limit on ducks at all when that picture was taken.

Robert Gardner's mother knocked loudly on the study door
then, and Robert quickly took the pistol that had killed his
father from the bottom of his father's gun cabinet, then
walked out of the house and got into his old Jaguar and started
the engine and drove down the long brick drive of the house
that was technically his house and out through the iron gate in
the brick wall that were technically his gate and his wall,
without ever even thinking goodbye. With cold November
rain dripping through the ragged top of the Jaguar onto the
passenger's seat and floor Robert Gardner drove steadily and
almost without thinking, his mind set into a fierce undis-
turbable autopilot, until he found himself on the road nearly to
Blue Mountain Beach, seeing for the first time the giant
monolithic and horrendously ugly mausoleums rising from the
dunes and knowing with epiphanic clarity that he had come
now to the sea in autumn on a fool's errand because it was the
only errand, error or not, that he cared anything about anymore forever and that the house at Blue Mountain Beach was
the only place in the world where he had any chance at all of
finding Dianne Bishop again, and the only place in the world
where he had any chance at all of finding Robert Gardner
again either.

Robert Gardner dreamed that night. He slept in the big double bed in the front corner room he had once shared with

Dianne Bishop, slept hard and long and deep despite the dank, musty odor of the linen and the staleness of the air in the house: a damp, sour, basement smell that seemed to linger even after he had unshuttered the windows and opened them all as wide as he could without letting in the rain.

In his dream Robert Gardner was young again and full of that immeasurable resilient energy that is not the mere essence of youth but youth itself. He was swimming and splashing around in a gentle, rolling surf, and while he was playing he could see his parents arguing on the beach. He could not quite hear what either of them was shouting, but he thought it strange that his father was wearing a business suit and carrying a briefcase. He saw his mother tug at the briefcase and after a struggle take it away from his father. She took a huge black pistol from the briefcase and Robert saw the familiar, silent, walled-up look come over her face as she fired the pistol into his father's chest over and over and over again until there was nothing left of his father but the burst insides of a huge red watermelon lying scattered about the beach. His mother turned the gun toward Robert then and said, quietly, "I won't lie for you again, Bobby."

The only thing Robert Gardner could think of to do, in his dream, was to run. He was grown now, or at least no longer a child, and when he started to run his feet sunk ankle deep into the wet sticky sand and soon his body began to feel very heavy and slow, so that no matter how hard he tried he never seemed to get any nearer the huge white mausoleum at the end of the beach. In a while he came up behind a group of soldiers running and soon he was running beside them. They were barefooted and had no helmets, but they were dressed in clean brown uniforms with very stiff creases and red epaulets, and they were all carrying black rifles. The last soldier Robert overtook had his father's face and said in his father's voice, "You've stayed too long, Son." Robert tried to say something in reply, but the words would not come out because every gasp of air that came into his lungs was scalding hot and burned in his chest with a fire that Robert Gardner knew was the same fire a man who shot himself in the heart would feel.

He had to stop running to catch his breath and stop the hurting, and when the soldiers ran past him now they all had grinning skull faces. They held their black rifles with white bony hands and the sharp bones of their feet scratched at the sand the way birds do when they scratch for feed. Robert turned around then but his mother was gone and Dianne Bishop was standing at the edge of the water painting a picture of three men shooting ducks from a small boat that seemed very far away. She looked very young and beautiful, but before Robert could tell her so she asked, in that perfectly full husky voice of hers he remembered so well, "Can a coward be a brave man too, Bobby Gee?"

That was all he remembered. He woke up with those words in his head and his T-shirt and shorts and both sheets soaked with sweat. When he opened his eyes the paneled room was flooded with sunlight but it was very cold. Robert shivered while he went to the bathroom to towel himself dry and put on fresh underwear. He took a sweatsuit and running shoes from his bag and put them on, then took the big army forty-five from the bottom of the bag and placed it on the nightstand. Still feeling cold, Robert closed the windows in both downstairs bedrooms and the kitchen, leaving the bathroom window in back and the living room windows that opened onto the porch in front slightly ajar so a cool fresh draft of sea air would ventilate the house. He boiled water on the stove and made instant coffee in a large Styrofoam cup. He had not remembered to buy milk, but the coffee was all he really wanted, that and a long walk now to shake the cobwebs out.

He walked down the steep steps which led to the beach, and in the cool freshness of the morning Robert Gardner was surprised how strong he felt. The dream had left him shaky at first, with the kind of hollow twisting in his gut that he felt when he had had one of the strong premonitions of disaster he had been having irregularly since he was eleven years old and, while sitting quietly in Sunday school, had realized with absolute unshakable certainty that both his parents were going to be killed in an automobile accident that very afternoon. That did not come true of course, none of them ever did, but they made him feel bad the way remembering the dream made him feel bad, so Robert finished his coffee quickly and began a long fast walk down the beach.

As he walked he watched the waves with the birds flying low down over the tops of them searching for small helpless fish caught in the relative maelstrom of the gentle surf, but Robert had understood for a long time that the constant merciless workings of the food chain were no more constant or merciless than the sun or the sea, which could both kill too, and he never felt sorry for the fish or the birds or for any animal in nature as long as it was not diseased or in a cage.

The surf was clotted with the same coarse brown seaweed that littered the beach. The sand was packed from the rain and the flat part he walked on, up away from the surf, crunched and squeaked beneath his shoes and the morning sun felt warm and pleasant on his face. He passed several people who were walking the other way, all very friendly though older than he, and they spoke to Robert in such crisp, clear Canadian voices that he thought he was imagining it until he remembered that many Canadians come south to the northern Gulf Coast in the fall and winter and the early spring to take advantage of the low off-season rates and mild weather.

He remembered the snows of their first Calgary winter, over a hundred inches in all and no record at that, and thought of Dianne Bishop teaching him to ski and the two of them laughing together on long walks, stopping at drifts and falling spread-eagle back against the banks to make snow angels, then kissing; later making frantic, hurried love with as many of their clothes on as they could leave on and still make love because neither of them ever learned how to properly bank the fire in the big iron stove before going out.

When he came to the small ria that had bordered the house Dianne had rented that first year, Robert looked up and the house was gone. He wished he had had the courage to look up toward it sooner because where the house had been was a four-story condominium of beige stucco and smoked glass that was exactly like five other condominiums that stood beside and behind it on both sides of the ria looking to Robert Gardner depressingly like six big microwave ovens. He stood and stared at them for a long time, wishing he had never seen them, and felt very bad when he turned to walk back to the house at Blue Mountain Beach.

He walked slowly, because now it seemed to Robert Gardner that there was nothing left in his life worth hurrying for. He told himself he had known the house would not be there, and wondered why he had even come. He did not think he was doing badly handling the no-wife thing, yet knew he had been setting himself up for a fall by even hoping to find

Dianne Bishop again after all these years. Three bad things together, his father had said. No wife, no Dianne and no job, at least probably no job, the way he had just picked up and left Calgary without so much as a fare-thee-well to anyone. Of course, without the wife he could do without the job. Like father, like son, Robert Gardner thought, only he wished that he had the guts to slip out sideways like his father did. That was what Big Joe Clarke had called it. Joe was the kind of guy who could get away with saying anything to anybody and usually did. He was an avid hunter and the only real friend Robert ever made in Canada: none of the draft dodgers would have anything to do with each other and most of them had gone home long ago anyway. But Big Joe Clarke liked every-body and Robert liked Big Joe immensely, even though he made dumb jokes about Robert's father committing sideways and the last time Robert saw him was in the process of mov-ing to Moosejaw with Robert Gardner's wife.

Robert decided then that the bravery his father had shown fighting the Germans was in no way diminished by the fact that, after nearly twenty-four years of enduring the incurable physical pain of shrapnel near his spine and the unending emotional pain of a wife who would neither love nor leave him, his father chose what he surely must have seen as the peace of death over the hell his life had become. Robert understood suddenly and completely what his father had meant about getting past scared so that you had to fight or die, or maybe even fight and die; knew what his father may not even have realized he was saying then himself: that the only truly bad choices we make are those forced upon us because we've allowed a bad situation to go on too long. That's what the suicide note meant, Robert knew that now, knew too that if all of that was true, as he believed now that it was true, then it was surely true as well that a man who runs away from something bad that he fears and hates can be a brave man in his own eyes, and in his heart.

Robert Gardner then, walking slowly near the water where the wet sand was solid beneath his feet and where too he could more clearly see the flotsam and jetsam of yesterday's storm being drawn inexorably toward the sea from which we all came, accepted and at long last forgave his father for the thing he had done, then in turn forgave himself and walked on.

When Robert Gardner reached the beach in front of his house the weak November sun was already near the horizon and a warm breeze was stirring offshore. Gulls and killdees were bobbing and gliding on the wind, searching and calling and diving for food. Two small sandpipers played in his shadow, pecking furiously at the bubbling imprints his shoes made in the sand, searching for sustenance.

He stood there for a very long time, looking out to sea and thinking of Dianne Bishop, and when the sun seemed about to set on the house at Blue Mountain Beach Robert Gardner turned and saw her walking toward him, smiling, searching too.

How Love Is

Mama Dormin cried. Cholly brought her out onto the front porch to meet Dixie Dupriest, and before he could get the first word out of his mouth his mama plopped herself down on the glider and started to bawl.

"You sound like a air-raid siren, Mama," Cholly Dormin said, then, "me and Dixie's getting married."

"I know," Mama Dormin said. "I already heard. Folks are saying it's going to be the biggest gatheration of Is's and Ain'ts since Tarzan married Jane." Then she started bawling again. Mama Dormin was not unaware that the wedding of Tarzan and Jane had never been depicted on the Silver Screen, but that wasn't why she was crying. Cholly's late father had looked a great deal like Johnnie Weissmuller, and she could see the resemblance in Cholly now too, though in Cholly it came in a way that Mama Dormin knew only herself and maybe, and this was a big maybe to Mama Dormin right now, Dixie Dupriest would ever call handsome.

"I don't care about any of that, Mama Dormin," Dixie Dupriest said. Dixie was convinced that it didn't matter who you married, as long as you married for love. On the other hand, Dixie's father, an attorney known as Smiling Jack Dupriest, was convinced his daughter had lost her mind. Upon being told of her impending marriage to Cholly Dormin, Smiling Jack had immediately and in front of Cholly offered Dixie twenty-five thousand dollars and a year abroad to forget Cholly and find herself a man who wasn't poor and ugly both.

"That's because you're an Is," Mama Dormin told Dixie. Dixie made a face like she didn't understand or didn't agree. Mama Dormin had already heard about the twenty-five thousand dollars but not the rest of it, and even though she had to admit it seemed like a lot for Dixie to give up for a man who made eighteen dollars a week cutting down trees for Boss Bishop's sawmill, it still made her mad. "The river never did care what the creek thinks," Mama Dormin said.

"You're saying I ain't good enough for her, ain't you Mama?" Cholly Dormin said. "All this about Is's and Ain'ts and rivers and creeks. That's what you mean." Cholly Dormin, who had no known enemies and a great many friends, was known as one of the most even tempered men in Garrison. He was a lover of fun and of peace, a man so completely without guile that, Cholly knew, people often thought him a fool.

But this time it hurt. Garrison is a small town, close knit in the way that comes from generations of families living in close proximity on the same land and sharing enough of the same values and beliefs to get along. And being such a place, six of Cholly's friends had already come up to him and told Cholly what they thought of Dixie's daddy's offer. Let her take the money and then marry her next year, they each had urged, as if outsmarting Smiling Jack Dupriest would be that easy; as if outsmarting Smiling Jack Dupriest had anything at all to do with loving his daughter.

"Tell her what you told Daddy, Cholly," Dixie said. "About the pot."

"Yeah," Cholly said. He sat down beside his mother and put his arm around her shoulders. "Mama," Cholly Dormin said. He cleared his throat. "Me and Dixie loves one another. We don't either one of us care if we never have so much as a pot to pee in, we'll be happy."

"That's how love is," Dixie Dupriest said.

"Cholly used to wet the bed and blame it on his dogs," Mama Dormin said. "That's how love is."

So the wedding was set. Cholly asked Boss Bishop to be his Best Man and Boss, who had all but adopted Cholly Dormin after Cholly's daddy was killed in a logging accident two years before, said he'd be glad to. He asked Cholly if they were expecting a big turnout, and when Cholly said four or five hundred people Boss Bishop was not surprised. He told Cholly there couldn't be over two or three people in Garrison who wouldn't enjoy seeing Cholly Dormin get the better of Jack Dupriest. "Including me," Boss Bishop said.

"That ain't what this is about," Cholly said. They were in Boss's office, between the log yard and the sawmill. Between the coming and going of trucks and the scream of saws, it was not always easy to hear.

"Say what?" Boss Bishop said. He cupped his hand to his ear and leaned forward.

"Nothing," Cholly said, then, louder, "Ain't y'all some kin?"

"Me and Jack Dupriest?" Boss Bishop said. He leaned back and propped his feet up on his desk. "Not that I know of," Boss said when he had thought a moment. "I'm first cousin to Doc Dupriest and Doc's first cousin to Jack, but I don't think I'm kin to Jack or Dixie. It's hard to keep up with. Folks around here is inbred worse than goldfish in a jar.

"Anyway," Boss Bishop said, "as long as you and Dixie ain't kin. Cousins ought not marry."

"My mama and daddy was cousins," Cholly said then.

"First cousins?"

"They had the same great-granddaddy."

"That's second cousins," Boss Bishop said. "That don't count."

"Mama says it's how come I'm only half crazy," Cholly Dormin said.

"You ain't half of nothing, Cholly, and neither is Dixie," Boss Bishop said. "And you'd better remember that if you're going to live in this little town after you're married. The only thing would make the old biddies down at the Hysterical Society happier than seeing a Dupriest marry a Dormin would be seeing the two of you split up. Give them something to talk about for fifteen years."

"Yessir," Cholly Dormin said and went back to work thinking about Is's and Ain'ts and rivers and creeks, wondering what difference it made to a bunch of gossipy old women what he and Dixie did. Cholly was trying to get it straight in his head just what everybody was talking about.

"The main thing you have to do now Cholly is just show up here at a quarter of six tomorrow evening," Boss Bishop said. It was Friday night and the rehearsal was over. Dixie's twelve-year-old sister Darlene had stood in for the bride, but only after making it perfectly clear to everyone within shouting distance that never, not ever in her entire life even if she lived to be two hundred years old would she ever kiss Cholly Dormin, even on the cheek.

"It's a full moon," Cholly Dormin said. "We ought to all go coon hunting down to the Big Bottom tonight." He meant himself and Boss and his groomsmen: Dan Steel and Blind Billy Benson and Dan's half brother, Mutt Binders.

71

"Dixie can be late," Boss Bishop told Cholly. "But you sure as hell better not be." They were standing in the back of the church, in front of and below the old slave balcony. It had not been used in nearly ninety years, but at Smiling Jack Dupriest's request his housekeeper, Camilla Tate, and Boss Bishop's housekeeper, Queen Merry Walker, were busy sweeping the old cramped balcony out and polishing the hardwood pews. Smiling Jack was expecting a big crowd, important people from as far away as Washington D.C. and New York City, he had told Cholly and Boss and the gathered groomsmen only moments before.

"One last hunt before Dixie leads you down the old Bridal Trail, huh, Cholly?" Mutt Binders said.

"Bridal Path," said Dan Steel.

"Cholly, you get lost out there tonight and we'll all be in a fix," Boss Bishop said. "Especially with all these important people coming in from Washington Dee Cee and New York City just to see you and Dixie tie the knot." Though he had been known to refer to New York City as the "Hemorrhoid on the Hudson" and had never in his life given any Washington politician so much as the time of day, Boss claimed he did not wink at Cholly then, as Queen Merry alleged, and told Dixie the next day that letting Cholly go off hunting with Dan Steel and Blind Billy Benson and Mutt Binders and trusting them to get Cholly back on time had been like asking the Three Blind Mice to bell the cat.

Dixie told him love meant trust.

"How love is," Cholly Dormin was saying, kept saying, had said, according to Blind Billy Benson, at least two million times since he kissed Dixie goodnight in front of her Daddy's house after telling her he planned to spend his last night as a bachelor chasing dogs and coons through the wild, cold October wetness of the River Swamp. It was after two A.M. now, and Cholly and Dan and Blind Billy and Mutt were warming themselves at a fire they had built on a low, sandy ridge in the middle of the Big Bottom that was the middle of the River Swamp. Boss Bishop was home asleep. The Big Bottom was on his land, and Boss loved the swamp at night. But he didn't hunt what he would not eat and Boss Bishop would eat neither possum nor coon.

"Shut up, Cholly," Mutt Binders said. "I'm listening to the dogs." The low, haunting moans of a pair of coon hounds echoed through the swamp and seemed to be traveling away from the hunters. They had gotten a late start and released only Cholly's dogs: a bluetick male Cholly called Red and a redbone bitch he called Blue.

"Crossing the river," Blind Billy Benson said. Blind Billy was known to have the worst eyes and the best ears in Garrison. He was the same age as Cholly but his bad eyesight had kept him out of the war, and at twenty-five he had only recently gone to work in his father's barber shop and then only because his father had used his influence at the state barber college when Blind Billy had neatly shaved a large mole off the back of a free-haircut-seeking wino's head. But Blind Billy Benson could tell you the exact location of any barking dog or fired shot in the River Swamp. It was a reciprocal agreement his eyes had worked out with his ears, Blind Billy would explain when questioned, and point out that even the wino himself agreed the mole had looked like a tick.

"Them dogs ain't swam no river," Dan Steel said. Dan was laying dry sticks on the fire, one at a time. When you looked up through the trees you could see the full moon, but outside the orange circle of fireglow the swamp seemed cold and very dark.

"How love is," Cholly Dormin said. Cholly had run around with Dan and Blind Billy and Mutt since grammar school, and now that he was the first to be getting married, Cholly felt a need to explain to his boon companions what they were missing. He liked the way Dixie would tell people, "That's how love is."

"How is love, Cholly?" Mutt Binders asked. He had been doing this off and on all night, egging Cholly on and getting answers that did not always make a great deal of sense.

"Love is your wife letting you stay out hunting all night and then having you a hot breakfast and a warm bed waiting when you get home."

"Still swimming," Blind Billy Benson said. The dogs were not barking now, and the woods were very quiet.

"A warm what?" Mutt Binders said with a grin.

"Bed," Cholly told him and gave Mutt the evil eye with his glass eye. That always gave Mutt and everybody else the creeps, especially people who knew Cholly had lost his left eye when he was nine. Cholly had been trying to get a wooden airplane out of a tree by throwing a broom up at it, but instead of getting the airplane down the broom had hit Cholly handle-first in the face and cost him his left eye. Later, after they had taken Cholly to the hospital and the ruined eye had been removed, Blind Billy Benson had climbed the tree and retrieved the plane. When Billy brought it to Cholly that night Cholly had told Billy to keep the plane, but Cholly's father found it later, lying smashed forever beyond repair in the big ashtray by the nurse's station.

"How can the bed be warm if she's been up fixing break-fast?" Mutt Binders asked.

"I ain't swimming no river," Dan Steel said. "Not tonight. It's too damn cold."

"That's how love is," Cholly Dormin said.

"Suit yourself," Blind Billy Benson said. "They're Lover Boy's hound dogs anyway."

"Huh?" Cholly Dormin said.

"You ought to get you a black dog too, Cholly," Mutt Binders said. "Then you could have Red, White and Blue."

"I don't even hear my dogs," Cholly said. He had been feel-ing so good about the way things were turning out that he had momentarily forgotten Red and Blue. He had had them since he was twelve, and, except for the time he spent in the army during the war, they had been his constant companions. They even slept with him. It was Red and Blue that were falsely accused of wetting Cholly's bed.

"Your dogs swam the river," Blind Billy Benson said. He stood up and dusted himself off. Dan Steel put two more sticks on the fire.

"Couldn't have," Cholly Dormin said. "They wouldn't cross the river unless I told them to." This, as everyone pre-sent knew, was an outright lie that Cholly had been telling to protect his dogs' honor for years. It was based on Cholly's father's firm and absolutely wrong belief that no raccoon was strong enough or even smart enough to swim a river that wide and that swift. Cholly therefore assumed, the first time Red and Blue swam the river after a big coon, that they had simply become lost, as Cholly himself often did.

"They're a good half-mile downriver now," Blind Billy Benson said. "You want me to go with you, Cholly?"

"Damn," Cholly said, then, "Yeah. Yeah, Billy, I do." But Cholly and Blind Billy Benson did not swim the river that night, they borrowed a boat. They hiked down to the edge of Cypress Slough and, with the help of the full moon and the carbide miner's lamps strapped to their heads, soon found the pirogue Doc Dupriest used to get into his duck blinds when the water was high.

"We can't cross the river in this," Blind Billy Benson said. The pirogue was wide and sturdy but could not have had more than eight inches of freeboard on dry land. Cholly assured Blind Billy Benson that he had been in the boat himself with not only Doc Dupriest but Jericho Walker and two of Doc's retrievers and at least a thousand decoys.

"But y'all didn't cross the river," Blind Billy said.

"No, but we run the edge clear around Pineapple Bend," Cholly told him.

"Well, I guess it might beat swimming," Blind Billy Benson said. He was helping Cholly turn the pirogue over and slide it into the water. They were very near the river.

"Strap your light up high on that dead cypress," Cholly Dormin said. "So we can find our way back if Dan lets the fire go out." Cholly considered himself an expert on thinking up ways to keep from getting lost, a skill he had worked hard to develop since running away from home at the age of five and discovering, to his dismay and eternal embarrassment, that his internal compass or gyroscope or whatever you wanted to call it was, in Cholly's words, about as dependable as a dead rooster.

"If Dan Steel's there, there's going to be a fire," Blind Billy Benson said. He had waded out into the slough and stood with each foot on a cypress knee while he strapped his

lamp to the tree. Cholly paddled the pirogue over to pick
Blind Billy up.

"That's what I mean," Cholly Dormin said. "The way Mutt
was grinning when we left, I expect they'll both be long gone
by the time we get back." Cholly had been expecting something all night long. Dan Steel and Mutt Binders were two of
the best friends Cholly had in the world, but neither one of
them had ever been able to resist what they called a good
joke. The trouble, as Cholly well knew, was not with the jokes
they thought up separately but with the opportunities that presented themselves to both of them at the same time. Little
things like slipping Limburger cheese into his coat pocket
before a deer hunt didn't bother Cholly, but sometimes they
could get right down mean.

"They're not going to leave us here," Blind Billy Benson
said, then, "they better not."

"See do that other paddle fit your hand, Billy," Cholly
Dormin said. "Blue sounds like she's halfway down to Mobile
already."

Cholly and Blind Billy Benson crossed the river in Doc
Dupriest's pirogue without a major incident, though the current in the middle seemed to grasp the buoyant little boat with
a vengeance, spinning it around despite their efforts and caus-
ing them to strike the far shore more than a mile below where
they wanted to be. Blind Billy Benson's lamp had become a
tiny white speck and Dan Steel's fire had disappeared completely.

"Hell of a note," Blind Billy Benson said.

"Can you hear the dogs?" Cholly asked him. They stood
quietly and listened. Cholly thought he heard them, but the

moon kept going behind the clouds and every time it did the wind rustled the dry autumn leaves.

"Smells like rain," Blind Billy Benson said.

"Sounds like they're way upriver," Cholly said. "Barking treed."

"Near Cypress Slough," Blind Billy said. He did not say this very loud, so it took Cholly a moment to grasp the significance of what he was being told. Cholly liked to tell people that he had only been provoked into a fistfight twice in his whole life: once during World War Two and the time Dan Steel and Mutt Binders stole his glass eye. It matched so well that Cholly had been able to fake his way halfway through the war with it, Cholly told people, until he got sand behind it on Utah Beach during the Invasion of Normandy and a master sergeant saw him washing his eye in his mouth. That the sergeant actually remembered to report it was what amazed Cholly, with all that was going on that day, but before he was transferred back to a desk job stateside Cholly had sought the man out and whipped him soundly, tossing him through the glassless window of a meatless butcher shop in a town called St. Mére Eglise.

And after all that, Cholly would tell people, to lose the thing because Dan Steel and Mutt Binders thought it would be a good joke to steal it from the water glass Cholly kept on the floor by the bed when he slept at Boss Bishop's camphouse, well, that was more than a man could take. Mutt hid it in the woodpile to scare Queen Merry Walker when she went to gather wood to build her morning fire in the cookstove and Queen Merry, who Boss told Mutt and Dan after Cholly whipped them had said she never thought it was a haint anyway, had smashed Cholly's glass eye to pieces with a five-pound axe.

"Across from Cypress Slough?" Cholly said. "You mean they're straight across from where we just come?"

"Right near the Meat Stand," Blind Billy Benson said. The Meat Stand was a tree on a bank which overlooked a deer crossing and had produced venison steadily and reliably for many years. The Meat Stand was also, as Cholly Dormin and Blind Billy Benson both knew, less than a twenty-minute walk from the place they had found Doc Dupriest's pirogue.

"Billy," Cholly Dormin said. "You're a good man. If I was to ever have a brother and got to have any sayso in who it was, I reckon it'd be you. But I do believe that right now me and you's gonna fight."

"You're not mad at me, are you, Cholly?" Blind Billy Benson said. He had told Mutt it was a stupid idea, that Cholly would never believe his dogs had crossed the river, but Cholly had believed it and Blind Billy Benson had found himself stuck in the middle.

"You was going to leave me here, wasn't you, Billy?" Cholly said. It was very dark now; the moon was hidden by clouds. The light from Cholly's headlamp was so bright it hurt Blind Billy Benson's eyes. It flashed off his glasses as he and Cholly circled the boat facing each other, each of them wading in and out of the cold water.

"I told them it wouldn't work," Blind Billy Benson said.

"Well you was right," Cholly told him. "Ain't none of you or all of you put together going to mess me up with Dixie Dupriest."

"That wasn't it," Blind Billy Benson said.

"Take off your glasses, Billy," Cholly told him. Cholly had stopped circling now. He was standing knee-deep in the river and Blind Billy Benson was on the bank.

"Then you take your eye out," Blind Billy Benson said. "I'm not fighting anybody with a glass eye."

"I ain't got the box," Cholly said. It had taken Cholly over a year to find a replacement that matched as well as the eye Queen Merry Walker axed, and he was not about to just stick it in his pocket now.

"Where is it?" Blind Billy Benson said.

"Back at the house."

"Well, go get it then," Blind Billy said. "And if you still want to fight, well, I'll be there."

"You'd better be," Cholly told him.

"I will be," Blind Billy Benson said. Then, in a flash of inspiration he would tell people later was either brilliant or stupid but not both, Blind Billy said what must have been the only words in the English language that would have calmed Cholly down. "You just keep an eye out for me, Cholly," Blind Billy Benson said.

Of course there was no fight, not after that. Cholly was late for the wedding, though, but only because Mutt Binders and Dan Steel were supposed to drive Cholly to the church so Dixie and Cholly could leave straight for their honeymoon in Boss's Buick instead of having to fool with Cholly's old truck, and Mutt and Dan honestly forgot to pick Cholly up. Or at least they said it was honestly. Nobody quite believed them.

And Dixie and Cholly made a pretty couple, too: Cholly with mud on his shoes and pants cuffs from walking to town through the woods and Dixie with that big smile of hers that was almost exactly like her daddy's, but pretty on Dixie.

Even Smiling Jack Dupriest seemed happy. He had all his important friends around him and he knew their seeing a man as important and wealthy as Boss Bishop stand up for Cholly as Best Man could not have hurt his reputation any. But that wasn't the real reason Smiling Jack was so happy that day. Most thought it was; everyone but Dixie's mother. She knew the real reason.

"When we were driving home last night Jack told me he's never seen Dixie so happy," Georgia Dupriest told Mama Dormin at the reception. "You can't imagine how much that means to me, to both of us."

Mama Dormin dabbed the corner of a napkin behind her glasses and looked at Smiling Jack Dupriest. "Ain't that how love is?" Mama Dormin said when she saw the tears in Smiling Jack's eyes. "Ain't that just exactly how love is?"

End of a Season

The deer the old man killed that morning was very large and had strange, knobby, convoluted antlers which no one had ever seen anything like before. He called it luck, but everyone knew the old man was a good and patient hunter who usually killed with one shot. They also knew he had used up his luck long before and now had to rely on other things. When they had gambrelled the buck at the camphouse they hooked it to the scales and were not surprised to find it weighed nearly one hundred and ninety-five pounds field dressed.

"Would have gone two-forty," one of the men said. Several others mumbled agreement.

They unhooked the scales and strung the deer up to be skinned. The old man cut the antlers and the top of the deer's skull off with an old, rusty handsaw.

"How many points you going to call that, Captain?" one of the young men who had begun skinning the deer asked.

"Eight point," the old man said.

"Looks like thirty or forty, if you count all those buttons."

"Seven and a half years old," a tall, neatly groomed man said. He had removed half the deer's lower jaw and was looking at it closely.

"You can tell that from his teeth, Doc?" the boy asked.

"Um-hmm. The way the dentine wears. He was an old man for this swamp."

"Guess his luck ran out, Captain," the boy said.

The old man gently shouldered the boy aside and quickly finished the skinning with a small, sharp knife. He worked with skill and determination, and in minutes he was done. He left the deer hanging to cool and put the strange antlers in his truck.

"One more drive?" Doctor Ross Dupriest, local physician, asked. It was late in the afternoon and he knew they would be rounding up dogs well into the night, but it was very near the end of the season.

The boy who had been skinning the deer had already climbed into the old man's truck. He knew that the old man they called Captain, because of a short-lived battlefield commission he had received during World War Two, would put him on a good stand and not try to save the best for himself, as some of the others would.

It was late, with barely an hour of daylight left, when they got to their stands. There was a short wait in the too-quiet winter woods. Leafless trees sighed in the gentle evening breeze. A loon called from across the river and, suddenly, dogs were barking and drivers yelling and whooping and then it was over too quickly. Near dark the boy heard a solitary shot from a big gun, very close, and knew the old man had killed a second deer.

The Captain was not without respect for the law, but he had hunted many days without even seeing a deer, and no one had ever been able to convince him that the one per day limit did not mean on the average. He whooped until the boy heard him and understood that it was too late to drag the deer out and that he, the boy, must get the old man's truck and drive in to get the old man and his deer.

The moon had not come up yet, and it was cold and clear and very dark when the boy and the old man finished loading the deer into the truck. The old man opened the door and took a plastic flask from behind the seat. He poured whiskey into two Styrofoam cups he had saved from morning coffee. He offered a cup to the boy, and they drove slowly on the smooth dirt road toward the camphouse as the young man sipped his whiskey. The Captain had finished his in two swallows.

"How many you got, Captain?" the boy asked.

"Six," the old man answered quickly.

"This your best year?"

"Close to it. You got one yet?"

"Yessir. Two."

"Good deer?"

"Got an eight point, stalk hunting up at my Grandpa's place, and a little spike over at Chenango."

"Bunch of outlaws over there."

"Yessir," the boy said, grinning. "Guy I go to college with invited me."

"Your granddaddy and his brothers used to hunt that land," the old man said, remembering.

"Yessir. You did too, didn't you?"

"Before the war."

"Must have been pretty tricky, getting around in the River Swamp without four-wheel drive."

The old man grunted a laugh, then said, "Mules."

"Kind of slow, wasn't it?"

"Had to leave town by midnight to get to the camphouse by dawn."

"It's not but nine miles."

"Mud."

"Oh, I forgot. The road wasn't paved."

"Not till 1954. Could have walked it faster, if we'd wanted. We needed the wagon to get the meat home, if there was any. Not near as many deer in this swamp then."

"When did you first start coming to Doc Dupriest's?"

"After the war, when Doc's pa let him start having hunts. Old Doctor Duncan didn't like anybody here but family, and not even all of them. We built that camphouse in the summer of 1948 or '49, but when hunting season opened the river was out and we had to leave the mules at the Possum Den Well and come in by boat," the old man said as he drove the truck around to the back of the stilted, unpainted old house that was belching thick, pleasant-smelling clouds of hickory smoke from three of its six mud-chinked chimneys. He backed the truck toward a thick, rough oak table which was made into and between two huge water oaks, each as wide at the base as the bed of the truck. Several men were standing around in the harsh light of two huge, bare bulbs. They were drinking from paper cups and talking, admiring the four skinned deer hanging from oak limbs thick as elephant's legs. When the old man stopped the truck they gambrelled the deer and were already skinning it when Doc Dupriest came out of the camphouse.

"Deerslayer," he shouted in a too loud whiskey voice from the top of the old, hand-hewn stairs, then let the door slam behind him hard enough to shake the porch screens halfway around the house in both directions.

"Old Cap teaching you to hunt, Bobby?" Doc Dupriest asked the boy, who was finishing the skinning while the old man sawed at the deer's six-point rack.

"Yessir. I guess so."

"Well, there's worse teachers."

"Yessir," the boy said and grinned.

"Him and your granddaddy used to hunt together a lot."

"Yessir."

"I remember them coming down here after the war. Hunt all day, fish all night. Wouldn't go home unless you made them."

"Yessir. Grandpa's told me."

"Reckon he'd be here today if he wasn't half dead."

"Yessir. He's pretty low."

"You tell him I said we'll be looking for him down here next year."

"Yessir."

"Damn good hunter," Doc said sadly and mostly to himself.

The old man grunted and cracked the last bit of bone to free the antlers from the skull.

"You come down here anytime we're hunting," Doc said to the boy. "No need you being mixed up with that Chenango bunch. Somebody's going to get shot over there. They put their standers too close together and shoot at anything that moves."

"Thanks, Doctor Ross," the boy said, without apology. A man hunts where he can.

Bobby folded the wet skin and laid it on the bloodstained table, where a man with two fingers on his left hand was butchering the meat. Several dogs had come in and were wandering around the camp. They were wet and tired and smelled like damp mops sprinkled with ammonia. The old man stood by the artesian well, and when a dog came to drink he would let it drink then pick it up gently and put it in the pen. He saw

Doc Dupriest put two newspaper-wrapped hindquarters into his truck and then divide the remaining meat among the other hunters. Soon only he and Doc and the boy, Bobby, were left. It was very quiet, and they could hear the low, mournful baying of a beagle deep in the swamp.

"I put your meat on the seat of your truck," Doc Dupriest said when the Captain came and stood beside him at the table.

The old man nodded thanks, and they heard the beagle bay again.

"Gigi's lost," Doc said.

"Any more?" the old man asked.

"Rasputin. But he'll find his own way home by morning. Gigi's the one I'm worried about. She's young."

"Need some help?"

"If you've got time."

"Time's all I got, Doc," the old man said with a faint smile.

"Bobby?" Doc asked.

"I'm with the Captain. Nobody's expecting me home early," Bobby said, then, "I'd like to help."

"Good. Thanks. Most of these folks can't wait to get home to supper. Sounds like she's heading toward the river, Cap. You and Bobby take the Broke Bridge Road up to the Possum Den Well. If you haven't seen her by then, get out and call her. I'll go down by the river. Blow your horn if you find her."

In the dark the old man locked the hubs of his truck and, for the first time that day, shifted into four-wheel drive. He poured himself another shot of whiskey, downed it quickly, then offered some to the boy.

"I've got my own, Captain," the boy said, producing a pint of cheap bourbon from the left front pocket of his camouflage hunting coat. The old man accepted the offer of a drink, downed it, and with the boy sipping from a paper cup they began a slow, tortuous drive along the road which ran diagonally away from the river, alternately crossing low ridges and disappearing into muddy sloughs.

"How come they call it Broke Bridge Road?" the boy asked.

"Because there's an old broke bridge across Limestone Creek."

"Everything's got a name."

"Yep."

The truck, though moving very slowly, bumped and tossed so badly on the slick, rough road that the boy spilled whiskey all over himself each time he tried to take a sip. He downed the rest quickly, then tossed his cup out the open window into the darkness behind the truck's headlights. They rode through tall stands of oak and hickory and pine that had not been logged since the twenties. It was dark there, even in daytime, but in the night there was a chill heaviness which was both peaceful and somehow oppressive.

"Hate to get stuck in here," the boy said.

"Yep."

"Or lost."

"Preacher got lost in here in '76."

"Which preacher?"

"Methodist. Bill Jacobs. Up in Tennessee somewhere now. Big, tall fellow. You remember him?"

"Nosir. I was with Pop in Germany then."

"That's right," the old man said a little absently, trying to remember the boy's father and who his people were. His memory was less reliable now, slower, though usually accurate. He had known the boy's mother all his life. Her father, the boy's grandfather, had been his friend for half a hundred years.

"How'd he get lost?" the boy asked.

"Who?"

"The preacher."

"Not paying attention, mostly. We had a late drive, like today, except it was hot and rainy. When we came by his stand to pick him up it was already dark and he was gone. We figured he'd walked back to the camphouse, only he hadn't."

"How'd you find him?"

"We didn't, not till morning. He kept moving around, wouldn't stay put. We'd hear him holler, and by the time we got to him he'd be somewhere else."

"Was that the night the snake bit you?"

"Yep."

"Rattler, wasn't it?"

"Yep. Big as your arm and seven feet long. Stepped right on him. Bit me three times before I could kill him," the Captain said, then reached under his seat and brought out a snakeskin bag tied at the top with thongs. He handed it to the boy.

"Open it," the old man said.

"Good God Almighty!" the boy said, loudly and slowly. He was holding a snake skull as big as his fist in one hand and seven inches of rattles in the other.

"You ever see a snake like that?" the old man asked, smiling.

"Nosir. Didn't know they got that big."

"They do."

"Grandpa said they nearly lost you that night."

"They did."

"Is that why everybody says you used up your luck?"

"Yeah, but it's not true. I've outlasted everybody but your granddaddy. I got some luck left."

"You used up a lot of it that night, Captain," the boy said, looking at the snake skull in the light from the truck's dash. He placed it and the rattles back into the diamond-patterned bag, tied the top, then tried to hand it back to the Captain.

"You keep it," he said. "I don't need it now."

"But it's your luck," the boy said.

"Now it's yours."

The boy put the bag into the right front pocket of his coat and held his hand against the bulge it made there. He thought of the strange deer the old man had killed that morning and of the whole long day and the warmth of the whiskey at the truck after they had loaded the last deer. The truck seemed to rock more gently as they got on higher ground, and the boy slept and did not wake when the old man drove through the creek by the broken bridge, nor when he first stopped at the Possum Den Well, which with its concrete trough stood at the corner of the big woods and looked down over two hundred acres of moonlit fields.

The silence woke the boy, or the Captain's gentle voice as he stood by the well and called the lost dog. He sat for a long time in the truck, looking out over the stubbled fields and at the wide, dark line the woods made between the earth and sky. He was half dreaming, half awake. He had not eaten since before daylight, but he was not hungry. The night was cold and already he could see a heavy frost forming on the stubble. He heard a short, hacking bark close by and got out to join the Captain at the well.

"Have a good sleep?" the old man asked the boy, who was washing his face in the warm water from the well's rusty steel spout.

"Um-hmm," the boy answered sleepily. "What time is it?"

"Past nine."

"Find the dog?"

"Doc blew a while back. Old Rasputin's close by. Thought I'd wait for him."

"Funny name for a dog."

"Doc never uses the same name twice. Ran out of regular ones a long time ago."

The dog barked, "Yowp." It was almost human.

"Heeere dog. Here dog. Here dog. Heere Ras. Ras, Ras, Ras, Ras, Ras. Heeere Rasputin," the Captain called loudly, with his hands cupped about his mouth.

"Yowp," the dog answered, closer now.

"He's coming in," the boy said.

"Maybe. Maybe not. He's getting old and don't hear too good, or acts like he don't. Mostly he just likes to stay out all night. He's the one found the preacher the night he got lost."

"How come you call it that?"

"What?"

"The night the preacher got lost."

"That's what it was."

"You got snakebit and almost died."

"You got some more of that rotgut whiskey you stole from your granddaddy?"

"Yessir. How'd you know I stole it?"

The old man took a long drink from the bottle, then handed it back to the boy. "Wouldn't nobody but your granddaddy buy that stuff," he said, then, "Heeere dog. Heeere Rasputin. Here Ras. Ras, Ras, Ras, Ras, Ras. Heeere Ras."

The boy took a drink of the whiskey, coughed, placed his mouth by the well's spout and drank some water, then took another drink of whiskey. He handed the bottle back to the old man and watched him finish it.

"Doesn't that stuff bother you?" the boy asked.

"I've tasted worse."

"Yowp. Yap, yap, yap. Yowp." The dog was running now, but away from them.

"Jumped a deer," the old man said.

"Must be a pretty good dog."

"Yep. He'll chase that deer till one of them drops."

"Yowp. Yap, yap, yap. Yowp." The sound was very distant and hollow, as if it were an echo and not the real sound.

"He's nearly to the river," the Captain said. "That old dog's going to drop dead one night."

"What's it feel like?"

"What?"

"Dying."

"What you asking me for?"

"Grandpa said your heart stopped."

"It started again."

"But what did it feel like to die?" the boy asked, a little too loudly. He was lightheaded from the whiskey and the empty stomach, but he was not drunk.

"Listen, boy. A man don't talk about these things. Folks are too busy trying to figure out the how of something before they've settled the why. But I gave you the snake, I reckon I owe you the rest of it."

"Yessir," the boy said. He sat down beside the old man on the low concrete wall. The old man was very quiet, as if gathering his thoughts. He smelled of musty denim and old, dry leather. When he had said nothing for several minutes, the boy spoke again.

"Captain?"

"Hush, boy. Listen to old Ras."

"Yessir," he said, and listened. And as he listened the boy found, in the cold quiet of the winter night, that he could hear the running dog and the chased deer and the owl at the edge of the big woods and the mice in the stubble of the field and a hundred other noises he had never heard before.

"You hear it?" the old man asked.

"I think so."

"That's what it's like."

"To die?"

"Close as I can remember. I was by myself when I stepped on that snake, and after I shot him in two I fell down and my carbide light fell in the mud and went out. It took them a while to find me because nobody knew anything was wrong, with just the one shot, except that the preacher was lost. I yelled, but they thought it was the preacher at first, and then my throat started to close up and I had to just lay there and take it."

"Weren't you scared?"

"No. You'd think you would be, but you're not. I just remember laying there in the mud and the rain and holding that dead snake's mouth shut so he couldn't bite me again while the rest of him was jumping around not knowing he was dead yet."

"That's funny."

"No. It weren't."

"They can bite you when they're dead?"

"Yep, when they're first killed. He was giving it a damn good try, too. I don't know how I got them, but when they found me I was holding his head in one hand and his rattles in the other."

"That's what Grandpa said."

"It's the truth, and it's true about my heart stopping, too. More than once."

"Then you died."

"A man don't die but once, boy. Don't let nobody ever tell you any different. When I was a boy the old folks used to say it was a big river, and that's what it is. It runs slow and deep, and you only get to cross it one time. I just got close enough to stick my toe in the water."

"But what's it like?"

"Dang it, boy. Be quiet and listen. It's just like right now. Everything is quiet and peaceful, and there's a brightness to the night that don't come from the stars or the moon. The longer I laid there the more I just sort of sank down into the mud, until I was almost part of it. I could tell where every man in the swamp was just by being part of the ground, and when my heart stopped the first time I knew it, and I could see your granddaddy and Doc Dupriest clear as day, even though they were half a mile off. And when I closed my eyes I could feel the swamp and the woods and the river, and I knew that a man don't ever die really."

"That's why you kept the snake's head and rattles, then. For luck."

"Not for luck, boy. To remember."

"Yessir," Bobby said, and placed his hand against his pocket to feel the cold, still hardness of the big snake's skull.

The Christmas Deer

Things were different when Cholly Dormin was a boy. Really different, Cholly says. The sun shone brighter and the air was fresher, especially in the fall and winter when it was cool and so crisp you could taste it. And he always got up early on Christmas morning too, Cholly did. Not that he found anything under the tree that kids today would consider special. Fruit mostly, and some things his mama knitted for him: sweaters and socks and maybe a scarf Cholly wouldn't wear. But there was always something there a little special, too. Cholly could count on that.

Not that the Dormins had any money. Hardly anybody did in the thirties. But they had a good farm and a solid house and barn that Cholly's grandfather built with his own hands, and they didn't owe anybody anything. The Dormins traded eggs and butter for coffee and salt; everything else they either raised themselves or took from the river and the woods. Cholly says he can't put a hickory log on a fire now without thinking of cold November mornings and hog stickings and his granddaddy's old smokehouse with its tight-chinked logs and gabled roof and two little chimneys.

And you know, if you're like the Dormins were then, with plenty to eat and a roof over your head and your family's healthy, it's a blessing just to be alive. But when you're a kid who's just turned twelve you don't know that, and you want things. Maybe your voice is starting to change or a little fuzz pops up on your face and you start thinking you're not a kid anymore, that you're ready for a man's things now. Whatever the reason, Cholly Dormin decided he was ready for a shotgun that year. He already had a little single-shot .22 that looked like a cheap BB gun and shot three feet to the left and a foot high at fifty paces. It only had one sight, on the muzzle, and learning to shoot that gun was what made Cholly the poor shot he is today. Or so Cholly says.

A man does need a shotgun, though, and Cholly had his eye on a twelve gauge L.C. Smith that Mr. Doyle Bryce had for sale up at City Hardware. Every time Cholly's folks took him to town, which wasn't but about twice a month, the first thing Cholly would do was go and look at that gun. He once even got up the nerve to ask Mr. Bryce how much he wanted for it, and Mr. Bryce told him fifty dollars in a way that said he knew Cholly's folks didn't have that kind of money. Cholly knew that too, he says, or should have, but he still kept looking at that big, beautiful double barrel every chance he got until the Saturday before Christmas.

Then it was gone. Cholly saw the empty place in Mr. Bryce's gun rack the minute he walked in the front door, and Cholly says he hasn't forgotten to this day how it hurt and how his heart just seemed to rise right up into his throat and push big, hot tears out of his eyes and down his cheeks. Cholly turned and ran back outside then, letting the door slam behind him so hard the cowbell bounced off its nail and hit the floor with a bang that made everybody in the store stop what they were doing and look at Cholly, and when they did Cholly ran and didn't stop till he reached the depot.

Cholly says he sat down on one of the outside benches to wait. He didn't want to go inside, didn't want to see people. He knew his mama and daddy had to pass the depot on their way out of town, and that was one Saturday Cholly did not want to get left and have to walk that long twelve miles home. Then he got the fidgets and decided that walking was better than sitting. It was too cold to sit, Cholly says, though it was a good, dry cold and not the wet kind that gets into old folks' bones. There hadn't been much rain that fall either, and Cholly knew his daddy would take the low road back, by the river, unless he had to take Mrs. Binders home. The ridge road was two miles longer, but Cholly's parents usually came that way into town, or at least they had since Cholly's mama's best friend Mrs. Binders divorced Mr. Steel because he went to town one Saturday and never came home and married Mr. Binders, who wouldn't go to town at all. Anyway, Mrs. Binders usually made her own way home, and Cholly headed out walking down the low road about as fast and lively as cold molasses, kicking every big rock he passed and throwing most of the little ones at the river.

"Stupid river," Cholly said. "Damn stupid gun," he said lower, and looked over his shoulder. Mama Dormin was hard on cussers. Said it was like calling the devil, and Cholly says he was just about to Dead Man's Slough then, where the road turns into the River Swamp, and Dead Man's Slough is no place to be calling the devil, not even in the daytime. Old Hick Johnson's granddaddy was dynamiting a beaver dam near there, back in the 1890's, and somehow managed to blow himself up with it. They never did find all the pieces and Cholly's grandmother and a bunch of other people claim they've seen strange things there in the dark of the moon. Looking for an eyeball probably, Cholly says. Cholly only has one eye, you know.

"Stupid Hick Johnson's grandpa," Cholly says he said right then, real loud. He was feeling pretty mean himself, and not particularly afraid of a ghost who didn't even have all his parts. Besides, it was a good three hours till dark. He climbed up into the big white oak tree that grows out over the river there, to wait for his mama and daddy and the wagon. He didn't much want to walk through the swamp by himself, so Cholly crawled out on a big limb and lay on it face down, contemplating the water and feeling depressed. He didn't hear the wagon, and when his daddy said, "Boy," real loud, Cholly jumped and almost fell into the river. By the time he scrambled down the tree and up into the back of the Dormins' old wagon it was already moving into the swamp.

"Stupid wagon," Cholly Dormin said, barely loud enough for himself to hear, then settled down to continue his serious thinking. Cholly says he knew he wouldn't have a minute's peace until he figured out what had happened to that shotgun. Somebody must have bought it, he thought, or more likely traded for it. There weren't ten people in Garrison who had fifty dollars spare cash in 1935.

Finally Cholly lit on the idea that his daddy had somehow, maybe by magic or mindreading or something, guessed how badly Cholly wanted that gun and had, with some sure enough magic this time, come up with the money to buy it with or found something he didn't need that he could trade for it. How in the world Cholly Dormin could think that a man who had but two suits of clothes to his name, one for church and weddings and funerals and the other for everything else, how Cholly could ever think that a man like that could or would spend fifty dollars, which was probably more cash money than he had ever had at one time in his life then, for a fancy double barreled shotgun for his twelve-year-old boy is beyond him now, Cholly says. He calls it optimistic stupidity, a severe brain disorder which anybody who knows him will agree has affected Cholly Dormin all his life. So try as he might, Cholly could come to no other conclusion than to believe his daddy planned to surprise him with that L.C. Smith on Christmas morning.

Well, Cholly was surprised all right. When he woke up it was just getting light and Cholly says when he stuck his head out from under the pile of quilts it was so cold in his unheated room off the front porch he could see his breath. When he realized it was Christmas morning Cholly jumped up so fast he forgot to put his socks on and yelped like a puppy when his feet hit the cold wooden porch as he ran across it to the parlor, where the stove and the Christmas tree were.

Cholly scrambled around under that tree then, looking for his one big present, but he couldn't find it. Cholly says he'll never forget that feeling, expecting something that wasn't there. Maybe that's the reason he still remembers that tree so well, though it sounds a little pitiful the way Cholly describes it, what with the way people do things now. But Cholly says despite the disappointment that was already building up in him that morning, that Christmas tree was the prettiest one he's ever seen: a big cedar strung with popcorn and a dozen real candy canes and the gingerbread snowmen and sugar cookie stars Cholly knew his mama had made and not Mrs. Santa like she always told him. On top was the same big star candle they had every year Cholly can remember but never lit because, though he didn't realize it then, if they ever lit that beautiful red and green and snowy-white candle there would have been nothing nearly so fine to top the tree with the next year.

Under the tree were oranges, real oranges, Cholly says, and bananas, too ripe but perfect for Mama Dormin's pudding.

Cholly's daddy used to say that when folks in heaven got together for Sunday dinner they served Mama Dormin's banana pudding for dessert. And six real, honest to goodness lemons were under that tree too, lemons Cholly's mama would turn into a pie nearly as good as her pudding. They only had things like that once or twice a year back then, Cholly says, and it made him feel good and happy to see all that bounty. Then he started looking for his own presents, especially the big one he still believed was there.

He found two pairs of wool socks his mama had knitted to replace the ones his big feet had outgrown in three months, and remembering his bare feet put one pair on and felt the warm, new-wool greasiness of them next to his skin. Near the socks was a new leather belt that was a foot too long, and Cholly put that on too, with the end tucked in and pulled right around his long johns. Still he found no long, narrow package, but there next to the tree's trunk was a suspicious-looking present wrapped in white tissue paper with his name pencilled on it. Cholly says he saw his mama and daddy standing in the doorway then, the one that led to the kitchen, but he didn't know how long they had been there. He tore the tissue off the present and, still kneeling, looked up at them and grinned. In his big hands he was holding two brand-new, shiny brass and dark blue paper twelve-gauge double-ought buckshot shells.

Now this is the part Cholly remembers best, or worst, as Cholly says. Because even remembering it now makes him feel a little sad. You see, when Cholly looked up his parents were smiling, and that was a rare thing. Life was too hard to always be smiling, Mama Dormin used to say. But they were smiling that Christmas morning. Cholly says that's the part he always remembers first when he thinks about that day. That, and how he must have hurt them, because Cholly could see that his daddy was holding a gun down by his side and even in the dim morning light Cholly recognized the chunky, ugly, rabbit-eared single-barreled twelve gauge which had once belonged to Cholly's grandfather and to Cholly's father in turn. Cholly thinks they must have seen the disappointment in his face then, because their smiles faded back to their normal hard expressions of determined fatigue before Cholly even reached for the gun. His daddy didn't say anything, he hardly ever did, but young as Cholly was he could see the hurt in the man's eyes and it made him feel bad. His mama just told him to be careful, which was about as much as she ever said about anything new Cholly wanted to try unless it was downright stupid. Then she got Cholly's daddy to make Cholly stop.

Well, even being just barely twelve years old didn't stop Cholly Dormin from deciding pretty quick that one barrel in his hands was going to do him a lot more good than any two that were still on the rack at City Hardware. Cholly says he dressed as fast as he could, grabbed his gun and his two shells, put a piece of the chicken his mama was frying for breakfast into the pocket of his coat to eat later, and without even slamming the back porch door left on his first deer hunt.

The sun was just starting to come up over the tops of the trees, and the mist from the river made eerie pools in the fields around their house. Cholly says he knew he was getting a late start and had to hurry, but he couldn't resist stopping to point and aim his new gun a few times, just trying it out, getting the feel of it, loading and unloading and pretending he was shooting. Then Cholly slipped his two shells back into his pocket and began a determined hike to the pasture. Cholly had seen deer tracks there, and his daddy had told him deer were slipping in at night to eat the winter wheat they had planted for their cows. Cholly's daddy thought deer were pests, though he would kill one if it got in his way when he had a gun with him. To Cholly they were and are big game: nervous, spooky brown ghosts you hardly ever see except as a flash of movement or shadow.

It was almost full daylight when he got to the pasture that morning, Cholly says, and from the low ridge he was on he could see cows already moving into the wheat. Cholly was at least a quarter mile from the far edge of the field, but he thought he saw a deer grazing close to the trees, all but hidden in the thin remaining mist. He stopped by a big cedar in the windbreak and stood completely still, watching, for a long time. The cold wind off the river began blowing toward Cholly and he tied his faded blue bandana carefully around his face, cowboy style, then went back to watching the motionless form near the woods that could have as easily been a clump of cockleburs as a deer. But it moved, Cholly says. Then it moved again and Cholly saw white antlers flash in a ray of sunlight. It made his knees shake and Cholly could barely breathe.

"Buck," Cholly says his brain told him then. "Be calm."

"I am calm," Cholly told his brain, but it knew Cholly was lying. Cholly says he was thinking fast then, looking, trying desperately to find a way to get within gun range of that magnificent animal still hardly distinguishable from cockleburs. The wheat they had planted in late August, which now stood between Cholly and his prize, was so gnawed and tromped on by their hungry cows that it was nowhere more than two feet tall. He could sneak up on the deer by walking two miles or so and coming up behind it through the woods, but Cholly knew that would take so long it would be gone when he got there. Of course Cholly also knew he could crawl through the stunted wheat with its thousands of soft brown booby traps, and since Cholly Dormin has yet to shrink from a distasteful task when the reward seems great enough, he dropped slowly to his hands and knees, fixed his eye on a tall hickory tree behind the buck, then lay prone and with his still unloaded gun began a patient, soldierly crawl through the wheat he hoped was hiding him.

Cholly says his imagination messed him up then, or his lack of concentration. Anyway, he became for a while a heroic doughboy crawling through the Argonne where his Uncle Nathan fought, until the sound of a fresh booby trap being laid and a loud moo brought Cholly home from the war. During his brief excursion to France Cholly managed to lose the fix he had on the tree behind the deer, and, since he didn't dare raise up to look for the deer, Cholly had to keep crawling and hope he was going in the right direction. But he wasn't. He came out in the woods a hundred yards from the buck and Cholly says he had never seen such a sight in his life, those huge antlers and the way the buck's neck was all swollen up like it had to be cutting off the blood supply to its brain. Cholly didn't know that happens to bucks every winter when they rut. He knows it now though, says he believes it happens to teenagers all year long.

Cholly reached into his pocket for a shell then and was trying to force a cold chicken leg into the breech before he realized what he was doing. When Cholly finally got the shell into place, leaving the ruined chicken leg on the ground where it had fallen, the deer had still not noticed him. Cholly calculated that he was at least fifty yards out of gun range and knew, if he didn't do something pretty quick, he wouldn't have anything but manure-stained clothes to show for his trouble.

Now, as Cholly saw it, his options were limited. He could try to crawl close enough to get a shot, but Cholly says he'd had enough crawling to last him awhile by then. He thought he might sneak through the woods, which would have been a sound idea if Cholly had been an experienced hunter instead of a twelve-year-old boy with buck fever. That made Cholly's decision simple: he would charge the buck, yelling and screaming like Geronimo. Cholly says he knows now that a more experienced hunter would never have tried such a stunt, but if he had that old buck would have been on its way to the Great Rutting Ground in the Sky. With Cholly it was safe—startled, but safe. Cholly thinks he shot it in the antlers, and by the time his fever-fumbled fingers had forced the remaining shell into the chamber that deer wasn't anything more than a fond memory crashing through the woods.

Cholly says he will always believe his daddy saw the whole thing that day, too. Not that he ever told Cholly that. Mr. Dormin wasn't the kind of man who made his opinions known about very many things, especially when somebody had tried something hard and failed. Everybody's bad at something, Mr. Dormin used to say. But even if he hadn't been watching, Mr. Dormin could have guessed most of what happened just by looking at Cholly's clothes and seeing the way Cholly was walking up to him there at the barn, his gun and his tail both dragging the ground.

"Need any help?" Mr. Dormin asked. Cholly says he could swear his daddy was trying not to grin then.

"Nosir," Cholly told him.

"Miss him?" Cholly's daddy asked.

"Yessir."

"Reckon two barrels would have helped?"

"Nosir," Cholly answered honestly, and when Cholly looked up his daddy was grinning and twelve years old or not Cholly ran to him and hugged him there by their old barn on that bright, cold, clear December day that Cholly Dormin says will lay forever pleasant on his mind.

Dry Fall

'Twas autumn when the manfire burned
Where few men ever have gone.
Deep in the swamp men were than night
And the wind blew straight from hell.

With both men dead now and the two of them so unalike, Doc Dupriest's quiet good manners and clover-honey hair that never turned gray seeming so nearly opposite the fire and darkness of Boss, it is easy to forget they were not only once inseparable hunting partners but first cousins as well as the only grandchildren Old Granville Bishop ever had, so that for them and Loon and Jericho Walker to have been hunting ducks and quail from one end of Pineapple Bend to the other that day was as natural as sweat in August, and anybody who says Boss Bishop shot those men and then got Doc to lie for him could not have known either man and besides, as much as Boss hated trespassers, he never would have shot Loon.

Shimmery shadows roamed about
Circling the whispering fire,

As wild-eyed men cooked devil's brew
On a night dark as the grave.

This was in the early thirties. Boss and Doc had already inherited Pineapple Bend and divided it, Boss taking Cypress Slough and most of the hardwood swamp they called the Big Bottom: low, swampy land that was home not only to white-tail deer but beaver and bobcats and a very few panthers and alligators, and of course ducks and geese in season, and Doc choosing for himself the high, open land on the north side of the Bend, land with soil nearly as black as oil where the edges were filled with quail and dove and grouse in the woods and small, hidden ponds close to the river where ducks came, the ponds Doc and Boss would hunt together when they got too old to walk deep into the swamp.

A demijohn caught sparkling drops
Of the nectar poor men craved,
Filled then carried to a johnboat
Tied over in Cypress Slough.

They gave Jericho Walker his house, the house his people had lived in since Granville Bishop bought them and brought them to Pineapple Bend to help him work the land; Boss Bishop and Doc Dupriest gave Jericho Walker that worthless old house with the porch you could not even lay a shotgun shell on without having it roll off into the dirt of the swept yard, that house with its rusty tin roof that barely covered the kitchen and let in the rain and cold of winter just as it gathered the thick heat of summer; they gave him that old and worth-less house because he would have no other but with it they gave him the section of land around it, not on the river but good land that would make Jericho Walker rich should he ever sell it now, and they paid the taxes forever.

These men knew not whose wood they burned
Nor cared they were trespassing.
Yet each his shotgun, pistol and
Knife kept always close at hand.

There had been far too little rain that year, heat without sustaining moisture but even at that, even if Doc's cotton had made even half a crop there would have been no demand for it, for any of it, and even though he had already lost most of his money in the lean years after the Great War every year now he lost more of it. Even his medical practice seemed relegated to delivering difficult babies and treating emergencies for thin, hollow-eyed people who already owed him so much money they would not look at him, turned away while he treated them until he would, exasperated, say for God's sake stop worrying about what this is costing, pay me when you can. At home he drank his lab-made, ersatz gin and worried himself.

Late at night they would hear strange cries,
The voice of a loon or hound,
And say loup-garou, *a spirit*
Undead in some beast must dwell.

Even Boss's lumber mill was only running two and three days a week then and that only to make bridge timbers for the state contract he had inherited from a mill upriver in

Tuscaloosa which had gone broke doing the same thing, so that for the first November since they were boys Doc Dupriest and Boss Bishop had all the time they wanted to hunt. They took Jericho Walker with them too, Jericho and Loon, the big yellow and gray God-knows-what-kind-of dog that Boss said looked like a cross between a possum and a shetland pony, that ran coons at night by himself when Jericho forgot to tie him and bayed treed the way a loon sounds at dusk.

> *Loud shots boomed out that whole last day*
> *From many guns, near and far;*
> *While drops of nectar smoothly flowed,*
> *The hunters hunted their game.*

They shot ducks at a pond near Cypress Slough that morning, wading in behind Jericho Walker and Loon in the darkness before the dawn, dragging feed sacks filled with old carved and painted mallard decoys, following closely behind Jericho and Loon because only the two of them could, had done it many a night, cross the Big Bottom in darkness needing no light nor compass nor moon; Jericho because he was the best hunter among them and Loon because he was Loon, retriever of ducks, pointer of quail, treer of gray and red and black squirrels and jumper of rabbits as well, whose only fault was that he would only hunt for Jericho Walker, run rabbits only past Jericho and maddeningly, especially to Boss who was not called Boss without reason, innocently and maddeningly would Loon bring any downed bird, no matter who had shot it, directly to Jericho Walker.

> *Near shots at morn, farther past noon,*
> *Thudding echoes filled the swamp*

And wild-eyed men cooked devil's brew
While the wind rose up from hell.

In the heart of that long day Loon hunted quail for them, finding six coveys as quickly and easily as if they were marked on
some secret map he carried in his triangular yellow head and
then, each time Jericho had stepped beyond his point to bust the
covey and after Loon had retrieved the downed birds, brought
them to Jericho who would pocket them or pass them to Boss or
Doc, infuriating Boss and Doc laughing at Boss's ire, each time
then if there were singles near enough to hunt and not scattered
wildly about the woods and grassy fields, then Boss would tell
Jericho to make Loon hunt singles and Loon would hunt them
slowly, lethargically, as if he had no idea what he was actually
supposed to be doing until he would stumble onto a single quail
as if by accident then point, yawn, and loudly break wind.

As day grew late the guns drew close,
Boomed somewhere near the river,
And each man checked his own guns' load
Then placed them close by the fire.

Late that afternoon, Jericho still out front but Loon dragging
and Doc carrying the one bag of decoys, they went to the river
for ducks, hid squatted in a canebrake with only a handful of
bobbing decoys before them, Jericho calling with a piece of cane
he cut and hollowed, sharpening the end with his knife and cutting two grooves near the other end and then calling a flock of
mallards down that they each took two of and then two wood
ducks that Boss killed with two quick shots from his ten-gauge
and then Jericho, as Boss and Doc watched, stared at him,

unloaded his old single barrel twelve and blew through the muzzle until a lone high-flying Canada dropped down and by the time Jericho had loaded and shot Loon was already in the water.

The swamp lay soundless now at dusk
Though these guessed not the reason,
For they knew not that owls should call
Or whippoorwills be singing.

Boss said he smelled mash cooking. They were walking in darkness, that early darkness which at first seems darker than the hour before dawn, walking along the treeless ridge called the River Road and feeling more than seeing the trees and water around them. Boss stopped when he spoke, whispered; he stopped then Doc stopped and Jericho stopped ten paces ahead with Loon. Doc said go on, Jericho, told him it was swamp gas that Boss smelled, said we've five miles to go to the Possum Den Well and ought to leave the chasing of *feu follets* and *loups-garous* and other strange things to Loon and Boss said, whispered between clenched teeth, that any half-Cajun son of a bitch who called himself a doctor ought to be able to tell the difference, but he did not say what difference, he just stopped suddenly, and Loon bayed.

Wild-eyed men heard the haunting cry,
The call of a loon or hound,
And said loup-garou *calls to us*
From deep in the swamp, or hell.

They all saw the fire now, glowing way off back in the swamp, an orange pulsing circle low in the trees, not the blue rolling flames of swamp gas but the fire a man would make or lightning from a storm if there had been one. With the smell though Boss knew what it was and said, lowly, whiskey, goddammit they are making whiskey on my land, as he walked down off the ridge into the waist-deep water of Cypress Slough, striking out straight for the fire with the four ducks tucked in his belt floating up under his coattails and splashing rhythmically; Doc telling Jericho even as he and Loon were already stepping down into the water, follow him, not bothering to say because if we do not Boss may kill those men. Jericho knew that.

Out of the darkness he was there,
One with eyes wilder than they,
And wild-eyed man drew down on them,
Both barrels loaded and cocked.

Boss stepped out into the circle of light the fire made and stood there alone, not speaking, silent until first one bearded, overalled, wild-eyed stranger saw him and then the other, separated from their guns and staring slack-jawed into the cavelike bores of Boss's big double, stopping, saying no word themselves but waiting, helpless, then watching Boss fire once into the center of their still, exploding it, sending a steaming geyser of heated mash spewing out from its side and then running down onto the fire and extinguishing it, bringing stinking steamy darkness upon them all while the strangers ran for their guns, or must have. Boss stepped behind a tree, Jericho and Doc stepped up beside him as Loon charged the wild-eyed men. There was shooting then, four shots: two men dead and Loon hurt bad.

Nectar spewed from their metal god,
Put the manfire quickly out.

A loup-garou ran between them
Then each shot at it and died.

They call that clearing the Whiskey Still now. Fifty years and more have passed and there is not even so much there as a piece of metal or glass from one of the demijohns Boss busted up that night, but you will still every once in awhile hear someone say they were hunting at Pineapple Bend and killed a buck near the Whiskey Still, and every time the weather turns dry some old codger is sure to start talking about the night the moonshiners died back in Cypress Slough.

A lot of people think Boss Bishop killed those men, too, but Doc said he did not and Jericho, who can be trusted implicitly when speaking about Boss, trusted that is by Boss, says the men shot each other when they were trying to shoot Loon, but Boss never said if he did or did not because the day never came on this earth when Boss Bishop felt the need to explain anything he had done to any man living and it is highly doubtful that when the time came he even gave St. Peter much more than a nod. He never would have shot Loon, though.

When the woods are dry in autumn
And the wind is in the north,
'Tis neither owl nor whippoorwill
That calls at night from the swamp.

From there the only sound you'll hear
When autumn is cold and dry,
Is the last sound two dead men heard
On a night dark as the grave.

That dog was hurt bad, too, took a full load of shot in his left side and lost an eye and the hearing in that ear, but Doc fixed him up that night and then came to Jericho Walker's house every other day for six weeks to check on Loon and to find out from Jericho if anybody had ever come looking for the two dead men, but no one ever did. Boss and Doc paid to bury them in the town cemetery and in a month it was like nothing had ever happened and Loon hurt was all there was to show for it.

Even he got better soon after that, went back to running coons at night by himself and baying treed exactly the way a loon sounds. He could not run rabbits any more, or not well, because if the rabbit circled left Loon would lose him. But he could still go to a covey of quail like a magnet to iron, even though Boss never again made Jericho make Loon hunt singles, and one day toward the end Boss waded out into a pond near the river to retrieve a duck from water he thought was too cold for Loon. Jericho forgot to tie Loon again that night and the old dog wandered off into the swamp for one last hunt. That was the last time anyone ever saw Loon, too, but someone hears him every dry fall.

'Tis neither owl nor whippoorwill
They hear calling in the night,
But an old dog who bays more like
The cry of a loon than hound.

And sometimes when you hear that cry
There'll be a glow in the swamp.
Some say it's men and some say ghosts
But none of them really knows.

Gathering at the River

When he was very young the man's grandparents had taken him to a baptizing at the river that ran by their farm. It had never occurred to him before that anyone could think of a river as a symbol of regeneration, but he would never again hear the old hymns they sang that day, "Shall We Gather at the River" and "Amazing Grace," without thinking of white-robed, smiling men and women rising up out of the water to shouts of hallelujah from the people on the shore.

His father had grown up on that river during the teens and twenties and early thirties, running bush hooks and trotlines from a heavy wooden johnboat and hunting when he could get shells for his .22 or the big, single-barreled mule of a ten gauge he shared with his younger brother. When he was six-teen he had taken two high-flying Canadas with a single shot from that gun and was very proud of that and of having killed a running rabbit with a one-handed shot from the .22 he chanced while juggling two stringers of fish.

So even though the man had come to prefer the hunting of quail and whitetail deer in the years since his grandparents and his father had died, he relished any opportunity to hunt ducks or geese and especially rabbits, though hunting them anywhere near a river made his heart ache.

This was another river then, thirty years and four hundred miles from that sunny summer Sunday morning he would never forget. It was February now, and this river was muddy and swollen from the winter rains. Deer season was over, and the men he hunted deer with had been invited to hunt rabbits on the land where they usually hunted deer.

He had traveled a great deal in his work and met many different people, and he thought these hunters among the finest men he had ever met. They would hunt in any weather and never complained when their luck was bad. They would never break any game laws intentionally, and the man knew that one of them had turned himself in the year before for accidentally killing a doe that had been running with the buck he shot.

They were not rabbit hunters, though they had all hunted rabbits at various times in their lives and in different ways. Like the man, they thought of it as a thing for boys or, on a cold February Saturday morning, as a diversion rather than serious sport. But the men who had come down from Tuscaloosa and brought the tiny beagles were rabbit hunters. The man did not know them, but he could tell from their seriousness and the shiny-clean coats of their dogs that these were men who knew the sport and loved it and that hunting rabbits with them in the River Swamp would be a very special thing.

He was not mistaken. They jumped the first rabbit thirty yards from the Five Spout Well, an old concrete cattle trough fed by the two remaining spouts of an artesian well that stands at the place where the narrow, muddy River Road leaves the fields and pastures and enters the swamps. It was one of the small hillside rabbits and the oldest member of the hunting party, a retired rural letter carrier and active farmer, took it with one shot from the old Browning he had taken many deer with one shot with too.

They hunted east, walking away from the river and then turning at the little clapboard church where some goats were staked out in the yard. They circled so that by mid-morning they had come to the lower edge of Limestone Creek, the place where the big woods start and the half-flooded bottom they call the River Swamp begins in earnest. The deer are bigger in there, safer and better fed. Rabbits are too. Big as possums.

After a break they crossed the creek. Everyone was weighed down with at least two or three rabbits and it occurred to the man when he was knee-deep in the cold, muddy water that in many parts of the world this creek would be called a river. When he was safely across he looked back to see the man who was the father of his wife and suffering from a rare and ultimately fatal blood disease that made it very uncomfortable for him to get wet, crossing on a precariously perched and slippery-looking fallen oak, and even though the old man was grinning from ear to ear the man breathed a sigh of relief when he saw him jump from the log to the creekbank. It would have been a thirty-foot drop.

They became separated there because it was so thick, with cane and brush and live oaks and hickory and cypress and gum all growing so closely together that the winter sun reached the ground only in faint yellow patches. No one could see to shoot in the thickets, but when they came out of them the man killed the first big canecutter he had seen since he had hunted with his father and his father's friends over the friend's dogs years before near a third river, and it seemed somehow very fitting that this time, as then, the size and unexpected quickness of the rabbit had caused him to miss and to have to wait for the rabbit to circle to take it.

"Did you get him?" one of the men who brought the dogs had shouted exactly as his father's friend had shouted that long ago morning, and he told them he did. He got him. The man slit the belly of the rabbit quickly then, as his father had taught him, and washed it in the river, for he was very close to the river now. When he slipped the long rabbit into the game pocket of his coat and felt the weight of it atop the two smaller ones he had taken up in the hills, his heart ached.

There was much talk when they stopped for lunch. The man had always thought that as a boy his father had been very poor, but some of the older ones there, including the man who was the father of his wife, had not even had single shot .22's and occasional bullets. They had hunted this same River Swamp with stones and slingshots and a strange, wonderful, coveted weapon called the knocker nut.

The man had never heard of it, and when he asked them what it was they told him you made a knocker nut by taping a large steel nut, of the kind found near railroad crossings and on certain pieces of farm equipment, to a stout length of hardwood, like the end of a broken hoe handle or a straight limb from a hickory tree.

He told the old men he could not imagine being able to kill a rabbit with such a thing, but they assured him a rabbit was easy enough to kill when a man was hungry. He believed that, the man told them, because he had been very young when his own father died and he had learned quickly that there are a great many things a man can do when he has to. He did not say it in a sad way, nor did he mean it sadly. But it seemed important that these men know he had been down for the count before too. More than once, though he did not say it.

In the afternoon they hunted the edges of the River Swamp. The dogs were fresh but the men were tired, and they had all taken several rabbits already. The man stayed near his father-in-law, and they talked in the way tired hunters will.

The old man told him that before the war they would come to this place in mule-drawn wagons, leaving town at midnight to cover the nine miles of muddy roads before daylight. He said he did not know if it was true or only seemed that way remembering, but the river would often as not be out and they would have to come in from the Possum Den Well, a well similar to and less than a mile from the Five Spout Well but on higher ground, in johnboats, and that there were very few deer back then.

He said that in 1948 or '49 several of them had helped the man who owned the land, father of the man and woman who owned it now, build the old stilted camphouse by the river in return for the favor and privilege of what had turned out to be a lifetime of hunting. He remembered a night, after the Rural Electrification Administration had finally gotten electricity out that far, when someone noticed dozens of rabbits sitting in the sedge and woods around the camphouse, helplessly hypnotized by the unfamiliar brightness of the lights. It was too much temptation for a bunch of ex-GI's to bear, the old man said, but the shooting had echoed out across the river and drawn the game warden to the camphouse as surely and quickly as the light had drawn the rabbits.

"Everybody was younger then," the old man said, and laughed. But his eyes said the world had been younger then too.

A year later, nearly two, when it was early winter again and the season for whitetail deer had begun, the man and the man who was the father of his wife and the grandfather of his daughter now, had stayed late in the woods when the old man had taken a deer in the very last moments of light before the darkness fell. When they had taken the deer to the camphouse and the old man had skinned it and sawed off the horns, they shared a drink of scotch mixed in two of the coffee-stained cups the old man kept jammed between the dashboard of his truck and the windshield. The whisky tasted of the smoke of a thousand campfires and faintly of coffee and was warm from the water of the Camphouse Well. They spoke little while a man with two fingers on his left hand butchered the deer, and it was dark and very late when they left for town.

A Hunter's Moon had risen, and the fields and woods near the Five Spout Well were as bright with elusive shadow as the first silver moments of dawn. They stopped there for water and another small drink, and the night seemed cold and very quiet. They did not speak, and above the gurgling of the well they heard the sound of voices singing, coming from the church on the hill. The words of the hymn and even the melody were indistinct and very pleasant as they flowed out over the fields and the woods and the swamp to the river, and the man would always remember thinking then what a fine thing it would be to live forever.

Three in the Bushes

"Beatitudes," Cholly Dormin said. Cholly was sitting with his feet propped on the shoeshine stand and holding an empty Coke bottle up to his right eye.

"That's what I said," Blind Billy Benson said. "Right after the meek inheriting the earth."

"And not eating catfish," Cholly Dormin said. He set the bottle down by the footrest so he could watch Blind Billy Benson. Blind Billy's glasses looked thicker than the bottom of a Coke bottle, and Cholly was trying to figure out how he could see to cut hair, especially Boss Bishop's, who didn't have a whole lot of it.

"That's right, Cholly," Blind Billy Benson said. "And don't leave that bottle where somebody'll kick it off like you did last time." Blind Billy was trying to even up Boss's sideburns with a straight razor when he saw Boss watching him in the mirror.

"A good barber can shave a balloon blindfolded and not pop it, Boss," Blind Billy Benson said. Boss didn't move.

"Blessed are they that hast a honest difference of opinion," Cholly Dormin said. "For they shall be the reason that ugly women marries and poor land sells."

Boss Bishop grabbed Blind Billy Benson's wrist and said, "Cholly, will you shut up while Billy's flapping this razor around my head. There ain't no beatitude about buying land or marrying women, and I ain't no goddamn balloon."

"Maybe it was Proverbs then," Cholly Dormin said. "Or Leviticus."

"Shut up, Cholly," Boss Bishop said, and this time Cholly did. He could tell Boss was in no mood to appreciate the fact that folks in the Bible seemed to have a lot of the same troubles folks was having today. But Cholly did have to admit he couldn't remember any of those old guys betting their brand new 1952 Buick they could outshoot the best shot in town. Not that it was Boss's fault exactly, or Doc Dupriest's either, even though he hadn't had to take the bet. Cholly thought if anybody was to blame, it was the communists.

Because what had happened was that Boss had come into Benson's Barber Shop while Doc Dupriest was getting his hair cut, which was not very unusual considering neither of them had missed more than a couple of dozen Friday afternoon haircuts at Benson's since they were little boys and Blind Billy Benson's granddaddy sat them on a red padded seat he had made to fit over the arms of his barber chair and dared either one of them to move or even complain about being first or second. That seat still leaned against the corner by the door to the back room, and little boys still sat on it to get their hair cut on Friday afternoons and Saturday mornings, but not this Friday afternoon. Cholly and Billy and Boss and Doc had had the place to themselves.

"Got me a new shotgun yesterday," Doc told Boss when Boss sat down in the vacant chair.

"Yeah?" Boss said.

"Twelve-gauge Parker. Just like new."

"Yeah?" Boss said. "Where?" And it was when Doc said he got the gun from Doyle Bryce's widow that the fireworks started. Not that he had ever cared that much for the Bryces one way or the other, Boss said, but he didn't think you ought to take advantage of widows. Then Doc told Boss, and Doc was red in the face now, that he hadn't seen Boss stop the bank from foreclosing on anybody just because they were down and out, which Cholly Dormin knew personally was not the truth and said so.

"Shut up, Cholly," Boss and Doc both said, nearly in unison, then kept on arguing. Doc said Sally Bryce was a proud woman who had offered him the gun of her own accord because there was no way she could ever hope to pay his bill, and he took it. Said he had taken chickens and hogs and muscadine wine and even a cross-eyed mule once that farted blue thunder and couldn't plow except in circles and besides, he'd be damned if Granville C. Bishop or anybody else was going to tell him how to run his business now or ever, thank you, Sir.

Then Boss stood up and said he did reckon Doc had a right to expect to get paid, and when Doc came up out of his chair with shaving cream still on his neck Cholly thought he was going to see a fistfight for sure. The two of them stood there face to face, with Doc jamming his finger into Boss's chest and shouting how if Boss was so much in favor of socialized medicine why in hell didn't he sell out and move to Russia so he could share what he had with the rest of the communists.

Boss didn't like that. Boss said communism wouldn't work because it penalized brains and hard work, and besides, this was about a gun, not politics. Said he was glad Doc had been able to beat the Widow Bryce out of her dead husband's favorite gun, but speaking of communism, he'd be willing to bet that Parker wouldn't shoot one tiny bit better than his old L.C. Smith.

"That," Doc told him, "is like comparing your new Roadmaster to Cholly Dormin's old piece of a Ford truck just because they both have four wheels."

"Mine ain't got but three right now," Cholly Dormin said, and this time even Blind Billy Benson told Cholly to shut up.

Then Boss Bishop said that might be so, but he would bet Doc the L.C. Smith against the Parker that he could take two doubles with the L.C. Smith before Doc could with the Parker.

"Doubles on what?" Cholly said, but nobody answered him and Doc wouldn't take the bet. Said the Parker was worth every bit as much as Boss's L.C. Smith and his Buick put together. So Boss bet them both against the Parker, against Doc Dupriest.

"Quail," Boss Bishop said.

"My place," Doc said. "Tomorrow."

"That's Saturday," Blind Billy said. He was already wondering if he couldn't maybe close for half a day; make up something and put a sign on the door.

"Hell of a burden being the only barber in town, ain't it, Billy?" Cholly Dormin said.

"The best barber in town," Blind Billy Benson said, brushing Cholly with his whisk broom.

"Have y'all ever noticed how it ain't near as bright outside in the fall of the year?" Cholly Dormin said. He was trying to untwist the leashes on a brace of Doc Dupriest's English setters: a red and white bitch named Jeanne. d'Arc but called Dark and a black-spotted male named Thomas Gray.

"Angle of the sun," Boss Bishop told him.

"That, and them mare's-tails," Cholly said, pointing at the sky.

"Rain tomorrow," Boss said.

"And the birds won't hold today," Doc Dupriest said. "They'll be too busy trying to get their bellies full before the rain sets in."

"I've seen fish do that," Cholly said. "It's almost like they know it's going to rain before the sky knows it itself."

"They do," Doc told him. "Man's the only animal that thinks he's smart because he can build an umbrella, when the truth is he's just too plain dumb to get in out of the rain."

"Amen," Boss Bishop said. They had parked Boss's Buick on the dirt ridge they call the River Road, beside a recently harvested pea field of thirty acres, more or less. Doc said there were birds around the edges.

"Y'all about ready for me to turn these dogs loose?" Cholly Dormin asked. He had the leashes untangled but Thomas Gray's was wrapped around Cholly's ankle. Cholly was a hound-dog man, unused to handling high-spirited, nervous dogs like Doc Dupriest's setters. Cholly had seen Jericho Walker handle these same two dogs and two others besides with no leashes and very few words, and he wished Jericho Walker was here right now.

But this time, with what was at stake, Doc had said that if push came to shove he thought Jericho might not be able to resist helping the dogs steer the birds just a mite more into Boss's line of fire than Doc's. Boss told him that was bullshit and he knew it. Said Jericho Walker didn't give a flying hot-damn about white men's betting, wouldn't even gamble with them. But then Boss said he didn't care who they took along to work the dogs: Blind Billy Benson or even Cholly Dormin.

So Cholly got the job. Blind Billy Benson said he was afraid that if he closed up on a Saturday morning some of his regular customers might drive up to Tuscaloosa for their weekly trims. "I hear they got electric clippers up there," Blind Billy whispered, not adding that he had driven up there himself one Thursday afternoon to check out the competition. "And *Esquires*," Blind Billy Benson said.

"I seen a *Esquire* once in Atlanta," Cholly Dormin said. "Had drawings of them Various Girls in it."

"Vargas," Doc Dupriest said.

"Electric clippers interferes with your brain," Blind Billy Benson said. "Proven scientific fact."

"I reckon I ought to bring my gun along," Cholly said. "Just in case."

"No," Boss told him.

"No," Doc said.

Cholly turned the dogs loose, unclipping Dark first and then Gray. He ran the leashes through a leather game bag Doc had given him and knotted them around his waist. "Hunt close, dogs. Hunt close," Cholly shouted, and was as surprised as Doc and Boss when the dogs stopped to wait for him and began to hunt close.

"Luck to you, then," Boss told Doc. He snapped the old L.C. Smith shut and took off a few paces behind Cholly and the dogs.

"Luck, then," Doc said, walking to Boss's right but ten yards away. At that distance he knew it probably would not matter that Doc was left handed, but if they got any closer it could. It was one of the reasons Doc Dupriest had always preferred good doubles over any other type of shotgun: no ejected shells in the face; slightly clumsy reach for the back trigger, but you got used to that.

The dogs found a covey quickly and Cholly flushed them before either Doc or Boss was truly ready, but Doc was readier.

By turning and firing twice, Boss took one that came up nearly over his head. Doc took two crossing at thirty yards, firing once. It was mostly an accident; Doc hadn't even seen the second bird except as a blur at the edge of his vision, but it was the kind of luck which is better than skill and Doc Dupriest had learned long ago that a man presented with such a gift should do his best to keep his mouth shut and act humble.

"Damn, Doc," Cholly Dormin said. "That was a hell of a shot."

"Hell of a gun," Doc said, patting the barrels of the Parker.

"We here for talking or hunting?" Boss Bishop said. He had reloaded and was considering, for the first time, the fact that he had very probably made a serious mistake in betting against his cousin. Boss had always been able to outshoot Doc with a rifle any day of the week and twice on Sundays, but there was something in Doc Dupriest's blood, maybe the leftover something trickled down to Doc from Doc's father's father, Jacques Broussard Dupriest, the old Cajun punt gunner who Doc said bolted what looked like a small cannon to the bottom of his pirogue and sometimes killed as many as fifty ducks with one shot. Boss didn't know if it came from old Jacques or from somewhere else, but he did know it seemed as if his cousin had literally been born with a shotgun in his hands. Probably a nice double, Boss thought. Doc never could do anything with a pump or automatic.

"Hunt, Dark," Cholly Dormin said. "Hunt close, Gray. Hunt close." But they found no other birds in the edges of that field, nor in the larger cotton field which was separated from the pea field by a narrow strip of woods, the picked-over cotton stalks dry and bare and rustling in the rising wind. Cholly looked up and saw that the clouds had gotten thicker and a little lower. He told Doc the birds had probably moved up into the brush to scratch for worms.

"I don't think bobwhite quail eat worms, Cholly," Doc Dupriest said.

"They would if they was hungry enough," Cholly told him. It always amazed Cholly that two men as smart as Boss Bishop and Doc Dupriest were supposed to be could know next to nothing about things that really mattered. What in hell did a bobwhite quail care if it ate worms or peas or cotton seeds? Did Doc think they were some kind of damned gourmets that sat around planning out their next week's menu like that bunch of old biddies from the Historical Society? Only Boss called it the Hysterical Society because they had been trying to make a museum out of Boss's house for thirty years that Cholly knew of. But Boss or Doc either one didn't understand history or bobwhite quail or much of anything else, or so it seemed to Cholly sometimes, because Cholly knew damn well that neither one of them had ever had to worry about whether the cardboard in their shoes would last until they could find another box, or even missed a meal unless they wanted to. What Cholly meant, and he didn't try to say it then because he didn't think he could say it so it would come out the way he wanted it to, was that a man missed a lot by not being poor a time or two, or at least broke.

"You mean a worm in the beak is worth two peas in the bushes, Cholly?" Doc Dupriest said. When Cholly looked at him he saw that Doc was smiling, that he thought he had made a joke.

"Something like that," Cholly said. He kicked a deadfall, out of habit formed by years of rabbit hunting, and jumped backwards a good four feet when two quail thundered up out of the brush. He crashed into Doc and they both tripped over each other and fell to the ground. Boss Bishop raised the old L.C. Smith to his shoulder and fired two quick shots. Both birds fell into a blackberry thicket at the edge of the field.

"There's you two in the bushes," Boss Bishop said, then, as he helped Doc to his feet, "Even."

"For now," Doc said. He was no longer smiling. It had just occurred to him, as he sat there on the ground watching the two birds fall and feeling his stomach sink to his feet, that without even realizing what he was doing he had bet his personal and occasionally erratic shooting skill against Boss Bishop's luck; bet a shotgun he would probably never see the likes of again, not in a little town like Garrison, against a shotgun he didn't want and an automobile he didn't need. He had a Cadillac that was nearly new, and no one else in his family drove. And the worst of it was not what he had bet, the Parker had not really cost him anything but a fee he had never expected to collect, so it did not seem to have the value of something you paid cash money for or gave up something else you wanted so you could have; the worst of it was that he had bet anything at all against a man so naturally lucky Jericho Walker claimed he could roll a seven with one die.

The dogs brought back one bird each, and Cholly added them to the bird bag. "Y'all got one double apiece in under two hours, when some folks hunt their whole lives without getting a single one," Cholly told them then. "Y'all ought to quit and call it even."

"Even, hell," Boss Bishop said. He could taste victory, felt his luck rising up in him the way the river rose after the winter rains and ran over everything in its path, felt his luck rising up in him the way it had almost every time he had ever tried to reach beyond his grasp.

"No," Doc Dupriest said. "We have a bet."

"Hunt, then," Boss said. He was not sure that victory had a taste, but the anticipation of victory surely did. It was a little like wild honey, Boss Bishop thought, or ribbon cane: dark and strong and very sweet.

They ate lunch in a grove of cedar trees by Limestone Creek. The day had become overcast and gloomy, which was the way the men felt too, except Cholly Dormin. Cholly had learned not to worry. There was a place on the coast of France called Utah Beach where Cholly Dormin had learned the futility of worry and the true value of a good night's sleep. But he knew that Boss and Doc had both been too old and too rich to have to go to war, though Boss's son Jack had gone. Jack had been in Europe when Pearl Harbor was attacked; Cholly had been coon hunting all night and went straight to Tuscaloosa that Sunday afternoon and got in line to join the army. Jack had waited to be drafted, got married, and went to war nearly two full years after Cholly, to the Pacific. Cholly could not imagine war in the jungle, thought it must have been worse than the war he fought, if anything could be worse.

Cholly was sure Jack Bishop knew some things that Boss could never hope to know, knew that the things Cholly and Jack knew completely were nevertheless not the kind of things you could bring home and share like you could a Jap flag or a broken bayonet. Yet it was something of great value, all of it. Cholly knew that.

They had finished their sandwiches. The dogs were sleeping after eating the two cans of dogfood Cholly had been lugging around in the bottom of the game bag all morning. Doc and Boss were sitting against opposite sides of a big water oak that grew up and out and over the cedar grove and were nearly asleep themselves. Cholly was burying the trash.

"Didn't y'all ever wish you was poor?" Cholly said. Boss and Doc were not only half asleep, they had both learned that wisdom required or at least advised that they let Cholly Dormin's non sequiturs pass unmolested into the stratosphere. They pretended to ignore him.

"I mean, y'all both been rich all your lives, and right now you both look about as happy as them five quails you just killed."

"Un-huh," Boss Bishop said, thinking as he said it that to say even that much in reply to Cholly was probably a mistake.

"And the both of you would rather take a beating with Blind Billy Benson's razor strap than admit you were putting up when you should have been shutting up," Cholly said.

"The voice of experience," Doc Dupriest muttered, smiling.

"Un-huh," Boss Bishop said. Cholly finished burying the trash and turned his brain off. Let Boss and Doc worry about it, he wasn't going to. He lay down with his head on Thomas Gray's rump and went to sleep quickly, another important thing Cholly knew about.

Cholly woke up when he heard shooting, and he knew Boss and Doc had gone on without him. Hell of a thing to do, Cholly Dormin thought, leave a man asleep here right on the edge of the River Swamp where some big old water moccasin or rattlesnake or something could crawl right up and bite him on the face. Cholly hated snakes. When he was little people in his grandmother's church handled copperheads and rattlesnakes to prove their faith. They were always getting bit. Cholly told his grandmother there must be something about it he didn't understand.

So he decided to try and find the road. He figured if Boss and Doc didn't need him any more than to walk off and leave him for the snakes to eat, then he would just walk home. Leave those two jaybirds to wonder where he was for a change. But the trouble with that plan was, Cholly had gotten turned around and couldn't find the road. He found a road, all right, but not *the* road, the River Road. The road Cholly found was an old logging trace that meandered through the swamp without any real sense of purpose, seeming even to cross itself on occasion, going nowhere. But by the talent he was noted for, which was referred to as either dumb luck or lucky dumbness, depending on who you asked, Cholly Dormin found himself, within an hour, near the edge of the field Doc Dupriest and Boss Bishop were hunting.

"There's Cholly," Boss said lowly, almost whispering. He nodded toward the far edge of the field. "He don't think we see him."

"Sneaking up on us, is he?" Doc said, and grinned. "Guess he's sore about being left."

But Cholly wasn't mad or sneaking either. He was still lost. The field was more than a hundred yards across with a rise in the middle, and in the evening overcast Cholly had not seen either Boss or Doc or even yet realized that this field had any special significance over any of a dozen others he had seen that day. Dead cotton and sedge and cockleburs (it took good land to raise cockleburs, Doc had said earlier) and peas, and the big woods behind them. Always the big woods behind them. Cholly jumped when Boss fired his gun in the air to get his attention.

"Y'all like to got me lost," Cholly told Doc and Boss as he walked up to them. Dark and Thomas Gray sniffed Cholly's pants legs, then sat. Their tongues were sliding out of the corners of their mouths, dripping in the cool evening breeze. Cholly could see they had been hunting hard.

"Cholly," Boss Bishop said.

"Yessir?"

"When did you ever come to these woods and not get lost?"

"Been lost some," Cholly admitted. Like about ten thousand times. Boss once told Cholly he had about as much sense of direction as a fart in a whirlwind. Cholly didn't know what Boss meant by that.

"Look over there, Cholly," Doc said, pointing toward the edge of the field behind him. It was the cedar grove where they had eaten lunch.

"You need a compass, Cholly," Boss Bishop said. He took a worn silver compass from his watch pocket and handed it to Cholly. "Can you read it?" he said.

"I could in the army," Cholly Dormin said. "Only you didn't have to much on account of you just went where everybody else was going and tried to keep from getting yourself shot or blowed up."

"Ha!" Boss Bishop said.

"Rough, was it, Cholly?" Doc Dupriest asked.

"A mite," Cholly said and told them that the worst thing was the screaming. Said had they ever noticed that in all the newsreels they showed during the war, there wasn't any screaming. Told them that was because the newsreels were filmed without sound and then the gunfire and mortar fire and bombs and whatnot were added in along with the talking later. "Back in Hollywood or somewhere," Cholly Dormin said.

"I didn't know that," Doc Dupriest said. "I should have noticed that."

"Nobody does," Cholly said.

"I guess that makes this foolishness of ours today seem pretty silly to you, doesn't it, Cholly?" Doc Dupriest asked.

"Nosir," Cholly told him. "It don't seem silly. There ain't much to it, I reckon, but I don't know as I'd call it silly. Puzzling, though," Cholly Dormin said. They were walking and came then to the Possum Den Well, a concrete cattle trough at the corner of Boss Bishop's and Doc Dupriest's land. Boss sat down on the edge of the well. Cholly drank water from his cupped hands, holding them together beneath the metal spout. The well was artesian, the flow as old as the land itself. Around the trough, built around the well when Doc and Boss were boys, mud was mixed with the manure and urine of the cattle that watered there. It made the footing slippery and sticky and gave off a sickly sweet aroma.

"Cholly," Boss Bishop said. He was sitting on the rim of the concrete trough. "We ain't seen another bird since lunch. How you reckon me and Doc ought to settle this bet of ours?"

"Like I told you," Cholly said. "Just quit and call it even."

"Can't," Boss Bishop said, looking up at Doc. Doc was standing back out of the muck, wiping the stock of the Parker with his handkerchief.

"Can't just quit," Doc said.

"Let me tell y'all what I saw once," Cholly Dormin said. He sat down by Boss. Both of them had their boots covered with the watery mixture of mud and manure and urine. Happy as pigs in shit, Cholly Dormin thought, but he didn't say it.

"True story?" Doc asked. Cholly Dormin's stories were not known for acute veracity.

"Truer than most," Cholly said.

"Ha!" Boss Bishop said. "That's what I call an honest man. Tells you right off he's lying. Ha!"

"Let him tell it," Doc said.

Cholly took out his pocket knife and started whittling the gook from his boots. After a minute, still whittling, he said,

"Y'all remember right after the war, when my uncle up in Birmingham got me on at the steel mills?" They both nodded. They also both remembered that Cholly had not stayed there very long.

"Them furnaces was the closest I ever want to come to hell in this life," Cholly Dormin said. "Or any other." Cholly told them it was so hot there your sweat dried up before it could reach your skin. Said the only way a man could keep even a little bit cool was to wear a pair or even two pairs of heavy long johns under his clothes, then once they got soaked with sweat you could stand in a breezeway every once in awhile and get cool.

He told Boss and Doc that in the eight months he worked in the steel mills he saw two bad accidents. The first was when he was working on the tail end of a rolling mill, raking hot steel bars off the cooling racks and into bundling bins, steel so hot it would catch your boots on fire if you stood still on it, cauterized leather gloves into stiff, unworkable iron in half a shift.

"Men had to shove ingots into this big drawing machine that squeezed the hot steel into rod," Cholly Dormin said. "So hot up there they worked thirty minutes on, thirty minutes off." Used big steel rods to shove the ingots in, keep them from binding, Cholly told them and said he once saw a man step up to give one of the glowing hot, stove-sized ingots a shove and just as he did the ingot slid over onto his foot and dragged the man all the way through the drawing machine before anybody could shut it off. "Nothing left but hair, teeth and eyeballs," Cholly Dormin said. He wasn't trying to be funny. That was truly all there was left of the man.

"I've heard of that type of thing happening," Doc Dupriest said. "When I was in medical school there, in Birmingham. Terrible."

"I guess you're trying to make a point with this, Cholly," Boss Bishop said. He took a silver flask from his pocket and took a sip, a signal that for him the hunting was over for the day.

"But the awfulest thing I ever saw," Cholly said, continuing as if he had not heard either man, "including the war, was one night when I was working on a ladle crew and somebody somehow got about a teaspoonful of cold water in the bottom of one of them big ladles, and when they poured the hot steel to it, it blowed up just like a bomb. Killed four men outright; only thing saved me was being far enough back that what splattered on me didn't burn through my longjohns. Blowed a hole in the roof fifty feet long, and that roof's a hundred feet high.

"But the awfulest thing was what happened to this colored man they called Little Man Moss, on account of he was so big. Little Man was standing about ten feet from the ladle, and when it started to blow I guess he turned to run. Anyway, he got splashed all down his back and his clothes burned off him like they wasn't nothing.

"And he was dying. You could look at him and tell he was dying, but he didn't look scared, running around hollering with his clothes and half the skin on his back burnt slap off him and you had to know that Little Man knew he was dying, too. But you know what he was screaming, Doc?"

"I don't know, Cholly. I've heard people say some strange things when they knew they were dying. He must have been in shock, too."

"Boss?" Cholly said.

"I have no idea, Cholly," Boss told him. "Water? Fire?"

"Save my dick," Cholly Dormin said.

"What?" Doc said.

"Save my dick. He was running around holding himself and screaming, 'Save my dick,' until he fell over dead. Took him four or five minutes to die, and that's all he ever said."

"Man's last words were 'Save my dick'?" Boss Bishop said.

"Save my dick," Cholly Dormin said.

"Seems like a strange thing to worry about at a time like that," Doc Dupriest said.

Cholly smiled. He wiped his knife on his pants leg and kicked his right foot. Chunks of manure and mud flew everywhere. "Well, I don't reckon Little Man ever had hisself a Buick automobile to worry about," Cholly Dormin said. "Nosir, I truly don't believe he ever did."

Hunter's Home

It was when he first saw the deer that it all came back and then too that Mark Perril forgot everything else he had ever been or done or wanted to be or do, until he did not even know that for now he was as a boy again. That would come later. So much had come before.

They hunted near the river, from the camphouse Mark Perril had last seen twelve years before, gray and almost stately, covered with vines. It looked no different now, the broken boards not replaced and only the roof of thick cedar shakes new. He parked in the swept yard, and inside the main room Mark found young Ross Dupriest trying to start a fire in the big, double-hearthed fireplace. He barely recognized the son of his cousin's cousin. Twelve years is a long time in a boy's life, Mark Perril thought. Or a man's.

When Ross told him he was in medical school now, Mark could not help remembering the last time he had seen him, the day Ross had killed his first buck. He was a wild, shaggy-haired boy then, almost uncivilized, who after bringing the buck back to the camphouse had stripped off his coat and shirt and even his boots, though it was below freezing, then climbed up into the very top of the big chinquapin tree behind the camphouse while the other boys there filled a ten-quart pail half-full of deer's blood. Ross taunted them too, without fear but not all in fun either. They caught him there, five or six of them, older and bigger, and drug Ross yelling and kicking down to the ground, and by the time they had pinned him to the game pole all the blood was not from the deer.

"Remember when they bloodied you?" Mark Perril asked. Ross laughed. He was dressed in neat camouflage clothing. The shirt looked new, but the pants and hat were so old and worn they had personalities. Others, several men and three women, were coming in now dressed much the same. The only one of the women Mark Perril knew was Dianne Bishop, daughter of his father's long-dead sister. She was glad to see him, Dianne said. Others did too. One of the men asked Mark why he had been away so long. Mark did not try to tell him.

But the woods have not changed, Mark Perril thought. He and Ross led five hunters to their stands while a dozen more drove to the far side of Cypress Slough and walked in from that direction. He had asked Ross to come with him, a little unsure he could find his way, but once they left the small circle of civilization Mark was surprised and pleased to find how little the woods had changed. He used no compass to lead them, though they had to walk through leafless hardwoods so tall and straight the December dawn's thin light only reached the ground in patches, and the blackberry and ash and palmetto and cane grew so thick that in places he could not see a dozen yards ahead.

Mark used no compass, did not need one when the sun shone or the stars were out, though he always carried the heavy, cased Edgemark his father gave him. It was tied to a lanyard around his neck now and stuffed into the breast pocket of his field jacket. He wished he had bought a new hunting coat. Even with the insignia stripped the jacket did not belong here, in this place. The fast walking and the silence of the woods and even the thick, musty odor of the swamp made him wish he had come back sooner. He felt good now, but there had been a time when entering the woods, any woods, with a gun in his hand and men following him was the last thing he wanted to do again ever. He lived in the city then, for years, always in sight of buildings and streets and people, searching or hiding, even now he did not know which.

Using only the sun's glow and the lay of the sloughs and low ridges that ran diagonally back from the river like the spokes of a huge wagon wheel, Mark led the hunters toward the wheel's hub, which was Cypress Slough. Cypress Slough, which had once been the river bottom itself, before the flood of 1859, when Old Granville Bishop, great-great-grandfather to Dianne Bishop and great-great-great-grandfather to Ross Dupriest, had at the height of the flood seen what the river was trying to do and then helped it along with slaves and mules and plows and even dynamite until, finally, when the water subsided, Granville Bishop and the river together had made Pineapple Bend and added nearly ten thousand acres to the land he claimed for his own. Cypress Slough, which was near dead center of that hundred-odd square miles men since Old Granville Bishop's time have called the Big Bottom, which itself lays in the center of the hundreds of square miles of prime timber and hunting land they call the River Swamp.

It has not changed at all, Mark Perril thought. They walked past a dozen wood ducks, hens and drakes, floating in the brownish water of a small slough, dipping their beautiful combed heads into the water, oblivious to the deer hunters. That surprised some of the men, but not Mark. He had believed for a long time that animals, especially wild animals, had a sense of danger few humans possessed. He had often come within gun range of ducks while hunting deer. Once he was slipping through the woods on a clear, cold winter day, armed with only a little .22 pistol and tracking a bobcat that had killed a fawn near the camphouse. When Mark came to an opening in a stand of loblolly pines, a big tom turkey stood there staring at him. And the biggest whitetail deer he had ever seen ran alongside his truck for a quarter of a mile when he was leaving Pineapple Bend the day after hunting season. Mark clocked it at thirty miles an hour before the buck sped up and crossed in front of the truck, jumped a barbed-wire fence, then ran through the middle of a herd of Dianne Bishop's grandfather's cattle.

"You stop here," Mark whispered to one of the men he did not know, giving him the first stand. When the man just stood there, Mark added, "And hide. You can see a long way in here. Deer can too."

Mark Perril did not like to tell others how to hunt. He had never been able to judge, by looking at a man, how well he could hunt. Sometimes there was a hardness in the eyes, but even that could fool you. Once, years ago, Mark had taken a young boy, the son of a friend, on the stand with him. The boy's mother had insisted on dressing him in a bright red shirt, this was before hunter orange, and to make matters worse, the boy's father had armed him with a .410 that Mark was not even sure would kill a deer. The boy could not or would not sit still either, no matter how Mark begged or threatened. Mark had given it up for a lost cause and lit a cigarette while he sat listening to the dogs run a race some-where deep in the swamp when a huge buck crashed through an ash thicket not fifty yards from them, running flat-out with its head and tail down and its legs flailing like scissors so its white belly almost touched the ground, and before Mark could even get the safety off his own gun the boy had shot the deer squarely in the neck and rolled it, stone dead, right at their feet.

"Which way the dogs coming from?" the man asked as Mark and the others hurried away.

"East," Mark said, and pointed away from the river, toward the edge of the Big Bottom. "Into the wind. But you get still and watch. Some of these big bucks like to slip out before they even turn the dogs loose." And that's about the only decent shot you're likely to get, too, Mark thought. He hurried on into the swamp now, hiking quickly through the water-filled sloughs and up over the leafy ridges, spacing the other hunters at least two hundred long paces apart so they could not even accidentally shoot each other unless one of them was fool enough to leave his stand. Mark cautioned all of them against that and said he hoped they all would get their deer. Of course he knew that would not happen. Most would not get a shot at all, others would miss. The dogs did not literally run the deer, the deer were too fast for that, but the dogs could get in and root them out of the beds and hiding places or just scare them with their barking, so that by the time a buck passed through the line of standers it was usually running full speed through the thickest cover it could find, and the only chance you had to kill one was to pick an opening you thought the deer might run through and then make your first shot count. Mark had once, while he was in the army, nearly come to blows with a light colonel from upper New York state who kept insisting that hunting deer with dogs was about as sporting as dynamiting fish. Yeah, Mark thought; so is hunting doves in a hurricane.

Only Mark Perril and young Ross Dupriest were left when they came to the big walnut tree some called the Meat Stand. The old tree stood on a high point overlooking Cypress Slough and had, for as long as anyone could remember, been one of the most consistently productive stands in Pineapple Bend.

"This was part of the old riverbank," Mark said.

"Think so?" Ross asked. "After all this time?"

"Sure," Mark told him. "A hundred years is nothing to this old swamp."

"I'll wade in to the Whiskey Still," Ross said. "Dianne's going to put her standers along the east and south edges of the slough. The three of us will be right in the corner."

"Put him on the ground, then," Mark said.

"Yeah. Put him on the ground," said Ross. He grinned, then disappeared quickly into the swamp.

Mark Perril sat with his back against the walnut tree. He was surprised how little it had grown. Near its base he found the small number fourteen he had carved when he was fourteen and killed the big freak whitetail with Appaloosa markings and fourteen perfect points. He thought he had carved his initials there then too, carved them near the ground because he thought they would grow as the tree grew until one day, when he was a man, his initials would be very large and loom high above the head of anyone who took the Meat Stand. But he had been wrong.

The ground was damp and cold, but there was very little wind. Mark was a man's height above the dark, shallow water of the slough and could see, in places, for nearly a hundred yards. He was hot from walking but left his cap on and his jacket buttoned because he knew that as soon as he had been still for only a very few minutes the damp coolness of the swamp would make him cold. Too cold for snakes, he thought, and remembered the Thanksgiving morning Jericho Walker had gotten permission from Ross Dupriest's father to turn the dogs loose on the Dupriest side of Daisy Parker Hill. They had a big crowd that morning, nearly thirty standards who between them killed seven nice bucks the dogs ran down out of the Dupriest's soybean fields and into what the deer must have thought was the safety of the Big Bottom.

The hunters had to drag deer out through the Bottom because there was no way to get a truck into where four of them were killed, and Mark remembered how hot it was around noon when he put his foot down by a big cottonmouth moccasin that was thick as his arm and just lying there sunning itself in some palmettos, so that when Mark raised his shotgun and shoved the safety off and fired with one hand the snake had already raised its black, ugly, poisonous head up through the tops of the palmettos and Mark saw, as in a dream, the sun glint on the white opening cavern of the mouth and the fangs whipping forward and all of it coming toward him higher than his knee and not at the gun but at the man and then before he even heard the shot, if he ever heard the shot, seeing the head disintegrate and then not even feeling scared or anything at all until he sat down back at the camphouse and began to shake so violently the burning tip of his cigarette fell to the floor. Since then Mark had seen the same thing happen to men who had been in firefights. He always told them later, if they were his men or his friends, about the snake. That it was okay. That he had gone back into the Big Bottom and killed a deer that same afternoon. But it never changed anything. I'm glad it's too cold for snakes, though, Mark Perril thought. Damn glad.

It was then he first saw the deer, and then too he forgot everything else he had ever been or done or wanted to be or do, until he did not even know that for now he was as a boy again; that it had all come back or maybe never even really left him. That would come later.

He saw the antlers first, as he had always seen them first. They were tall and white and polished, moving with a jerky slow sureness through the canebrake between the Meat Stand and the small circle of dry land in the middle of Cypress Slough some called the Whiskey Still. He could hear the dogs yapping in muffled excitement deep within the swamp and knew they were far away. So the buck had been bedded down near the Whiskey Still and was slipping out of Ross Dupriest's way. All of this Mark Perril thought without thinking, as a good quarterback watches the whole field as soon as the ball is snapped. The deer was trotting now, running almost directly toward Mark with its head and ears up, and as soon as it broke free of the canebrake the buck lowered its head and increased its speed so the gap between it and the small ridge where Mark sat was closing unbelievably fast.

Mark knew the buck would not see him, knew a head-on shot was risky, but knew too because it had happened before that at the last minute or second the deer would swerve to avoid climbing the steep bank. So he chose an opening where he hoped the deer would run and, moving as quietly as he could because the deer would not look up now unless Mark made a sound, he eased the safety off his shotgun and held his aim at the small gap between two cypress trees. He would get one shot. It would be long, fifty or sixty yards, but if only one of the fifteen double-ought buckshot from his twelve-gauge magnum load struck the deer's neck or spine or even shoulder, that would be enough.

Mark was aiming left and the buck swerved right, leaping now. Mark swung over into a prone position and fired once at the buck's shoulder, rolling it into a blackberry thicket. Mark stood at once, pushed the safety on, and slid down the muddy bank into the slough. He had not gone ten steps toward the thicket when it began shaking, then he heard splashing as the buck ran out the other side. Mark felt sick. The deer had run off so fast he thought he might have only grazed it. Then he found a hand-sized smear of thick, dark, veinal blood where the buck had fallen and felt better. Mark hated to bloody a deer, had not done so but twice in all his hunting, and now did not believe he had done so again.

When he began tracking he knew. There was too much blood. The buck would crawl up into a thicket and die. If Mark could not find it, the dogs would. He was glad the deer was not gut-shot so it could run a long time. That was always bad. He whooped loudly so Ross Dupriest would know he was moving toward him. When Ross whooped in reply Mark knew he could safely walk around the blackberry thicket and enter the canebrake. He could not see three feet in there and the tight, close feeling of imminent danger bothered him greatly, though he knew it was false. He found a game trail, not eight inches wide; there on the cane was a smear of blood. Before he had gone another twenty paces Mark found the deer dead.

He whooped loudly so Ross would know where he was, then sat down in the low bowl of a triple oak to wait. The dogs were closer now, yowling and yapping and running through the swamp. He could hear the drivers too and smell the dry dusty sweetness of the canebrake. When he looked up through the treetops Mark Perril saw that the sky was that deep December blue which comes only in the late fall or early winter and marks the start of a time of very good weather. It's a fine day, he thought. Truly a fine day. And Lord is it good to be home.

Aground in Blue Water

The Albatross is a fishermen's bar. It's an old lapstrake building set on pilings near the edge of Blind Bayou, and nobody who could afford to charter Bill Kesmer's boat would be caught dead drinking there. It's the way it smells, kind of salty and sweet, like whiskey and sweat. It's loud, too. Fish talk, mostly lies.

Omar Hand spoke when Bill came in. Omar bought the Albatross after some dopers stole his boat. Since then he's acted like a pit bull with an attitude. He already looked like one. He said, "How's fishing, Jake?" Omar sounds like a foghorn stuffed with oyster shells, calls everybody Jake.

"For shit, Omar," Bill Kesmer told him. Omar set a double Cutty and water down without wiping the bar.

"Bad run?" Omar asked.

"Two half-days," Bill told him.

"Unh," Omar grunted. He knows that's four times the work of one all-day: in and out twice, cleaning up. "Somebody waiting to see you," he said then and nodded past the crowd at the end of the bar, toward the booths.

"Yeah?" Bill said. He took a sip of his drink, then leaned on the bar without looking around. It had to be somebody from the bank. He'd missed some payments on the *Maria*.

"I wouldn't keep a dame like that waiting," Omar Hand said. When Omar grins his mouth looks wider than his head.

"Dame," Bill Kesmer said and looked at him. Omar grew up with Bill's old man. Both of them talk like a Bogey movie.

"Yeah. In the back booth." He nodded again, still grinning. Omar doesn't get many women in the Albatross, not with any class.

Bill picked up his drink and walked back to see who it was. Lady banker, he figured. But it wasn't. It was Charlene, Charlene Dupriest. She looked up when she saw him and smiled, just the way he remembered. Charlene's short upper lip makes her look like she's smiling all the time, like she knows some big joke and won't tell you. Her hair was still blond, dyed maybe but pretty, even cut short. She seemed sadder, though. Her eyes and face were pale and bleached, like driftwood.

Charlene stood up and Bill kissed her, long and hard. People were watching. At least half of them knew Bill's wife; a few would recognize Charlene. Maria Kesmer would know all about it long before Bill got home, but that didn't matter. Not then. They sat down facing each other. Charlene sipped her wine; the gold on her hands and wrists sparkled in the candlelight. She said, "Hello, Bill," and Bill remembered her voice, how deep it was for a woman, even when she was twenty-one.

"Charlene," Bill said. He took a long swallow of scotch.

"You look great," she told him.

"You look greater."

Charlene said, "Thanks, Bill. It's been a long time." She started to say something else, but hesitated. Then, after a minute, she said, "The man at the marina told me I'd find you here." Bill had forgotten how Charlene could use her voice. She could compliment a man's clothes in a perfectly sincere way that would make him check to see if his fly was open.

"I come here sometimes," Bill said.

"What an odd little place," Charlene said, in the same tone. "Does it always smell like this?"

"The smell keeps the jerks out, Charlene," he told her and felt the hair on the back of his neck stand up.

"That's something you never called me, Bill," she said. "Bitch and whore, but not jerk. I don't think I like jerk." She looked at Bill and smiled.

"This is no good, Charlene," he told her.

"It's just like before, isn't it?"

"Yeah."

"Do you still love me?" she asked.

"Sure," he said.

Then she said, kind of low, "You never really did, Bill."

"I thought it was the other way around."

"I know," she said and smiled again. She was stroking the backs of his hands with her fingernails.

"Bitch," he said.

"Don't, Bill. You don't have to be ugly."

"Sorry."

"I shouldn't have left you like that."

"Then why did you?"

"I don't know," she said. "I thought I knew then. I did love you, Bill. That's God's honest truth. But I wanted to be somebody."

"Everybody's somebody, Charlene," Bill said.

"I mean with a capital *S*."

"Did you make it?" he asked.

"I don't know, Bill," Charlene told him. "Maybe. At least now I have money." Bill Kesmer laughed. Charlene Dupriest had been a summer girl, a doctor's daughter. Her father's boat was bigger than Bill's father's house; Dupriest land covered thousands of acres. Now she was rich.

"Look, Charlene," Bill said. "I'm tired. If you're after my money, I have twenty-seven dollars in my right front pocket. But don't let Omar find out or he'll make me put it on my bar tab."

Charlene looked at him, still smiling. She said, "I want you back, Bill." Bill laughed.

"I'm not kidding," she said.

"I never thought you were."

"You laughed."

He told her, "It can't happen, Charlene." Everybody in the place was listening. Omar brought Bill another drink and another glass of wine for Charlene. He was grinning again, ear to ear.

When Omar had gone Charlene said, "I've changed, Bill. Really. I've learned not to be a bitch."

"That just leaves whore," Bill Kesmer said. Charlene slapped him hard. Bill took his drink and walked through the crowd and went outside and sat in his Jeep. It was just getting dark; still hot and sticky. In a few minutes Charlene came out and sat beside him. They could hear fish slapping the water on Blind Bayou, and somewhere near them a big gator roared twice. The mosquitoes were awful.

"I'm divorced now, Bill," she told him.

"I'm not," he said.

"Didn't you marry that pretty little Italian girl, the one whose father had the grocery store?"

"Yeah," Bill said.

"Marcia, was that her name?" Charlene pronounced it Mar-see-uh.

"Maria," Bill told her, but she knew.

"Sure. That's right," Charlene said. "I remember now. I bet you've got a dozen kids."

"Four," Bill told her. He wanted to go home then, just crank up the engine and tell Charlene Dupriest or whatever her name was now to get her fine ass out of his Jeep and out of his life so he could go home and have another drink and kiss his kids and go to bed and make love to his wife and then maybe sleep straight through till four A.M. when he had to get up to go fishing again. But when Bill looked at her to say it, Charlene was crying. Even in the dim light he could see big tears running down her cheeks. Bill took her hand. She gripped his hard.

"Charlene," he told her. "I've got to go home."

"I know," she said. "Just stay with me until I'm okay."

Bill told her then, "No, Charlene. I can't." He walked around to her side and helped her out.

Charlene said, "I need you, Bill." She looked up at him, not smiling, as if she wanted to kiss: the way she used to look at him when she was lying.

"No," Bill Kesmer told her. "You don't." Then he left.

The drive did him good. The breeze off the Gulf had died, and it was hot even for early September. He drove too fast, spraying oyster shells into the palmettos and pines at every bend in the road, but going fast made the air feel cool when it blew around him. The outside lights were off when Bill got home. Maria had heard.

Maria has a temper. People think it's funny. She's half her husband's size and tries to beat the shit out of him every time

the moon's wrong. Screams at him in Sicilian too, like her
mother. She is pretty, though. Charlene was right about that.

"Charlene says you're pretty," Bill Kesmer told his wife.
They were in the kitchen. He caught her wrists when she tried
to hit him. She spat at his face.

"Come on, Babe," he said. "This isn't my fault. She came
looking for me." Maria spat in his eye. He held her hands
behind her back and pulled her close. He tried to kiss her then,
but she turned her face away. When he nibbled her ear she
giggled and relaxed. Bill let her go then, but it wasn't over.

"What did the whore want?" Maria asked. She was leaning
back against the sink, speaking English. Her eyes were red.

"She's not a whore, Babe," Bill told her. "Just an old
friend."

"You used to say she was a whore."

"She wasn't."

Maria stared at him. She said, "She screwed other guys."
The ends of her hair shook and her lips were white as sugar.

"That was a long time ago, Babe," Bill told her. "Forget it."
He reached for her, but she pulled away from him and stood
behind the butcher block, by the knives. Her face looked like
a summer squall.

Maria said, "She wants you back." Spittle flew. She put her
hand on a butcher knife. Bill tried to step past her to go back
outside, but she blocked his way.

He said, "Yeah. So what?" Then Maria hit him, hard. Bill
used to fight some, when they were first married. Bare knuck-
les mostly, side-show stuff for money that some hardasses and
highrollers put on over near Pensacola and Biloxi and sometimes New Orleans. You have to be pretty broke to do something like that, bare fists are bad, but you learn how to take a

lick so you don't come home with your head in a basket. Half
those hardasses couldn't hit you as solid as Maria can.

"Stop it, dammit," Bill Kesmer shouted. Maria spat.

"Goddammit, Maria. I didn't do anything."

"What did she say?"

"That she's rich now, and she wants me back."

Maria said, "She was rich before."

"Yeah. I guess she got richer."

"What about the guy she married?"

"They're divorced."

"Whore," Maria said, then spat.

Bill said, "You're going to have to mop the floor, Maria,"
then, "Drop it, okay? I'm hungry."

"You've been drinking," she said.

"I drink every night."

"Not with her."

"Jesus Christ, Maria. Will you let it go? She was waiting for me
at Omar's and we had two drinks together and I left, and that's all."

"You kissed her."

"Says who?"

"Manny says," she told him. Manny the Mouth, Maria's
brother. The kind of guy used to hang around the playground
and pick fights with kids littler than him. Talks all the time;
never says anything. Turned the store into a fish market after
their old man died. Most of the commercial guys sell to them,
for Maria's sake. They don't like Manny.

Bill said, "Manny wasn't there."

"Did you?" Maria yelled. She mumbled something in
Sicilian that Bill didn't understand. The vein on Maria's fore-
head was big as a pencil. She screamed, "Bastard." Bill was
ready and caught her hand.

"Why?" she said. She was calmer already, but she wanted an answer. "Why?" she said, again.

"I don't know," he told her. "I do not know."

Charlene Dupriest stayed in town. Somebody told Maria that Charlene and her kid had leased a condo out on Sand Key, one of those big, expensive jobs in a building that looks like a stack of burial vaults with windows and won't take the first square hit from a hurricane half the size of Betsy or Camille. Not like the Kesmer place. Bill's grandfather built it in the thirties, two miles inland and on a solid ridge so far above sea level it never even floods.

But that's the way that old man was, planned ahead. Taught Bill to buy good equipment if he wanted to catch fish, and then to keep it clean so the salt won't eat it up any faster than it has to. Said everything else was common sense and luck. Blue water was what the old man called good luck. Bad luck was running aground.

Friday, a week after the thing with Charlene Dupriest at Omar's, Bill Kesmer didn't have anything booked for the weekend, so he was aboard the *Maria* cleaning equipment and hoping for a walk-on. He was sitting on one of the fighting chairs with a twelve-hundred-dollar reel spread out in about twenty pieces on a towel on the other chair, when a skinny, freckle-faced kid with curly blond hair came up and asked about an all-day. Bill told him he doesn't take kids and the boy didn't say anything. He just stood there on the dock, looking at Bill. Bill said, "Kids and drunks break things."

"It's just me and Mother and my girlfriend," the boy said. He took a roll of hundreds out of the pocket of his windbreaker and counted off eight.

"Nine," Bill said. The boy gave Bill another hundred, then smiled like he knew some secret. Bill told him to be there at five in the morning with somebody over thirty and sober, or it was no-go and half the money. The boy looked around the *Maria* for a while, smiling. When he left Bill got back to work.

This is where things started to go bad, the next morning. Billy Kesmer was there, Bill's oldest son. He was eighteen then and had been going out with Bill as helper and then mate since he was ten, when he wasn't in school. Billy wants to be a fighter like his daddy; boxed Golden Gloves and never lost a fight. Bill told him losing fights is what turns good fighters into great ones, but Billy's too young to understand that. Anyway, he's a good kid and a hard worker. They had the *Maria* ready to go and were sitting in the fighting chairs drinking coffee when a white Rolls-Royce pulled into the lot. The skinny kid got out, then a young girl, then Charlene Dupriest. Charlene and the boy were both smiling.

The girl was young and pretty and half asleep. Charlene was beautiful. Bill got her some coffee and told Billy Kesmer to rig four lines as soon as they cleared the pass. That would keep everybody busy until they got to deep water; let them get used to the equipment before they got onto something important. Bill climbed up into the tower. You can see the channel better from up there, and you don't have to talk. A few minutes later Charlene climbed the ladder with a mug of hot coffee in each hand. She didn't spill a drop.

"Cream, no sugar," she said when she handed Bill a mug.

"Yeah," he said. "Thanks."

"Mad at me?"

"No."

"You've hardly spoken."

"Channel's tricky; low tide," he told her.

"Can we talk?"

"The mate's my son."

Charlene said, "Oh."

"He can't hear you up here," Bill said.

"Does he know who I am?"

"Yes."

Charlene stood in the corner by the rail and stared out at the Gulf and the red sky for a long time. Then she turned and looked at Bill. She said, "The sunrise is gorgeous."

"Means rain," he told her. "Red sky at morning, sailor take warning."

"That's depressing," she said. "Billy so wants to catch fish."

"Billy?" Bill Kesmer said.

"My son," Charlene Dupriest told him.

"Oh," Bill said, then, "Fishing's always good before a front moves through. Didn't your old man teach you that?"

"That was a long time ago, Bill," Charlene said. "This is the first time I've been deep-sea fishing in years. Billy's never been."

"Who's the girl?" Bill asked.

"Just a girl."

"She doesn't look like the outdoor type."

Charlene said, "Billy thinks they're in love." She was frowning. The way Charlene is, she has to try real hard not to smile when she says something serious or lies.

"What is it, Charlene?" Bill Kesmer asked.

"Billy is your son," she told him.

"That's right. William H. Kesmer, Jr. Everybody but his mother calls him Billy."

"I mean my Billy," Charlene said. "He's your son too."

"Bullshit. He's too young."

"He's nineteen."

"He doesn't look nineteen."

"He begins his second year at Emory next week."

Bill tied the wheel and turned to face her. He put his hands in his pockets so they would stop shaking, then told her, "Look, Charlene."

She said, "Okay," and smiled.

Bill said, "How do you know?"

"When I was in college, when you were driving up to Tuscaloosa every other weekend...Bill, I was seeing another man then too."

"You mean screwing another man then too."

"Yes," Charlene said, still smiling.

Bill said, "So one of us knocked you up, and you decided to give the baby a rich daddy."

Charlene said, "Yes." She was crying. Maria Kesmer cries all the time, but not Charlene Dupriest. It's the way they were raised. Maria's mother cries if the mail is late, but Charlene's mother was a cold bitch. Shot Charlene's dog once for peeing on the carpet.

"And you're sure he's mine?" Bill asked.

"My husband, my ex-husband, never produced a live sperm in his life. We found out when we couldn't have any more children," Charlene told him.

"So he divorced you?"

"No, not really. We stayed together until I caught him with the upstairs maid. That's the truth. Ugly little slut, too. His warped idea of revenge."

"Does the boy know?"

"About the maid?"

"No, dammit. About me."

"I'm going to tell him tonight, Bill. I wanted him to meet you first."

Bill said, "Jesus, Charlene. Why?"

Charlene said, "Because it's the truth."

Maria was sitting in her husband's Jeep when they docked. Someone was with her. It looked like Manny. Bill told Billy Kesmer to clean the fish, then walked over to the Jeep. He said, "What's wrong, Maria? The kids okay?"

"You been running around on my sister," Manny said. He was sitting behind the steering wheel, looking at Bill across Maria and talking through his teeth.

Bill said, "Shut up, Manny." Manny's spent his whole life just begging people to beat the shit out of him. Gets drunk at Omar's and calls everybody peasants, only the way Manny pronounces it sounds like pissants. Omar says he has a brain defect.

Then Manny said, "I'm going to whip your ass, you little pissant." Manny still thinks big means tough. He was talking for the crowd, though. They were all around them then, with Billy Kesmer right up front. Maria wasn't saying anything, not even looking at anybody. Manny got out of the Jeep and they squared off. Bill saw Charlene and the two kids standing back, leaning against Charlene's Rolls. Then Manny hit him.

He hit him quick and hard in the gut. Bill wasn't ready and it knocked the wind out of him. He shoved Manny back and Manny started dancing around on his toes, grinning. He came at Bill with his left and Bill let it glance off his chin. Then while Manny was off balance Bill popped him and closed his left eye. Manny swung again and that time Bill smashed his nose and closed his other eye. Manny couldn't see good by then and his nose was spurting blood all over the place, but he was still jumping around swinging and trying to hit Bill.

"It's over, Manny," Bill said. "Go home." Manny wasn't hurt bad yet, but Bill knew he had to stop it. And that's the way it ended, the whole thing, like one of those late summer storms that come up out over the ocean and growl and thunder for awhile but don't leave much rain. Billy Kesmer led his uncle away and the Rolls seemed to have disappeared into thin air. Bill and Maria were left alone on the dock and it started to sprinkle, raindrops hitting the water and the boats and the dock and making it all smell fresh and clean and good.

Maria Kesmer hugged her husband then, kissed his bleeding hand. "I guess we need the rain," she said.

"Not this much," Bill told her. "We never needed this damn much."

Lost

He had missed completely. Mark Perril, who was a good hunter though not yet in the habit of being alone, stood alone now in the first cold rain of the winter of his life and watched the buck he had failed to kill disappear into the wall of wet, black, looming hardwoods which began the River Swamp. "To hell with deer then," he said loudly but without heat. "To hell with deer and to hell with women. And goddammit to hell with all this losing."

The buck's tracks were easy to find, obvious, unhidden, not like the tracks of a wife who scrawls, "Mark don't come after me," in wide, purple lipstick letters on the mirror over her empty dresser and then disappears into the steel and concrete swamp of Atlanta without leaving any tracks at all. But these tracks today, Wednesday, four days and nearly three hundred miles from the city where Sheila had left him, from the city where Mark had called the agency which had been the only one to give him a job when he lost his agency and told them simply that he was taking some time off to go deer hunting, not that Sheila had left him or even where he was going: back to the woods of the River Swamp he had hunted alone as a boy and the only place in the world he felt like being right now; these tracks were easy to find: deep, splayed, cloven, the prints of a big deer running in mud and Mark knew he could follow them even in the rain.

He thought of his compass then, knew that no matter how good a woodsman you thought you were you should never enter the Big Bottom without one, even remembered stories of men who had gotten lost in there: good hunters too, like Mutt Binders who wandered around for over a week eating raw game and drinking the swamp water that gave him the black shits he nearly died from, or the Methodist preacher who was hunting with a dozen other men and still got so lost it took the rest of them all night to find him and even at that one of the others, a man called Captain, almost died from the three bites he got when he stepped on a huge rattlesnake in the dark. Mark had seen the fist-sized skull of that snake, held its dry, evil-looking rattles in his hand, and even thinking of it made him shudder.

Yet while he was thinking this Mark was moving toward the deer, easing his way into the edges of the swamp because he knew that if he hesitated in this heavy rain, took the time to go back to his truck and remove the old silver Edgemark his father had given him, untie the leather lanyard and attach it to his shirt or raincoat as he should have done in the first place, knew that if he took the time to do the one thing he absolutely had to do before following the buck into the Big Bottom that the rain might obscure the tracks and then he would stand a very real chance of losing this deer. "To hell with losing," he said again loudly, again without heat.

So he went on, told himself he was man enough and hunter enough too to find his quarry without getting lost and then forgot it, put failure out of his mind and walked deliberately into the swamp, moving quickly through the cold and the rain, wading waist-deep sloughs that soaked through his jeans and boots, rushing to pick up the trail again as soon as he reached the edge of each low, grassy ridge; stalking the deer, oblivious and for a time even imperious to the tall, dark army of cypress and hickory and oak closing in around him, limbs like old men's fingers shaking in the wind and rain around him while a thousand unseen animal eyes watched him walking deeper and deeper into the wilderness of the River Swamp, he thinking nothing but of the deer as he entered the deer's unchanging world, leaving far behind the world of constant senseless change Mark was not even conscious yet of leaving.

He sensed the buck's presence then, felt it more than saw it, flowing as smoothly silent as fog among the trees with only the tall, white brightness of polished antlers held high in triumph and daring to give it away. Mark quickened his pace. Ignoring the tracks now he trailed by sight, hurrying toward glimpses of shoulder or leg or antler already gone before he could even move toward them, chasing the apparition deeper into the swamp, oblivious not only to the swamp itself but to his own discomfort and even time; waiting, watching, following, thinking of nothing at all but the deer until in the middle of a shallow slough he caught his foot on a hidden root and put his left hand on the wet, dark trunk of a cypress tree to keep from falling and saw that his watch read half past two, that not only had he been trailing the deer for nearly five hours but that it would be dark in less than two. Mark blinked and looked around him then, felt and looked exactly as if he had just awakened with a hangover in a strange bed, wondering at first, looking around himself and knowing, then saying as loudly as he could force himself to speak, "Goddammit I am lost."

His words fell dead at his feet, seemed not to carry even so far as twenty paces to the next low ridge, yet when he had spoken a squirrel eating an acorn in the rain stopped to bark at him from a tall white oak in the middle of the slough behind him. Mark turned to look up at the squirrel and when he looked back down every direction seemed the same: black water and brown ridges and wet, black trees. The only green he could see was one small cedar by the edge of the slough and palmettos on the ridges, that and the brown-green moss that grew on every single side of the black oaks it favored, not only on the north. Never only on the north, Mark thought, not here, not this far south and so deep back in the River Swamp you can never see all of the sun, even at noon in winter.

A man has got to have a compass to find his way in here, he thought stupidly, and after he had waded out of the slough he sat down on the horizontal trunk of a tree he knew from the mud still clinging to its tangled roots must have been uprooted by the line of thunderstorms which preceded the rain. Only a fool would try to cross the Big Bottom alone, he thought, and a damn fool at that if he tried it without even so much as a compass in the rain, though he knew others who had done it. Jericho Walker roamed the whole River Swamp day and night without ever getting lost that anyone knew about, and no matter the time of day or night or what the weather was Jericho could always tell you which way the river was and how far. But as Mark thought he looked around him and realized that not only was he not even half the woodsman Jericho Walker was, he was so lost that he could no longer say with any degree of certainty which direction he had just come from or where the deer had gone.

To hell with that deer, he thought then, and I was not born here like Jericho Walker either, but if I will just stop being so damn stupid I should be able to get myself out of here alive or at least keep myself alive until somebody can find me. It was then Mark realized how completely alone he was, that with Sheila gone and no one at work expecting him back until Monday there was no one even to miss him, that it was only Wednesday and could be Friday or even Saturday before someone found his truck and even then they would know it was his truck, know he was a good and capable hunter who would never enter the Bottom alone and without a compass, so it could be as late as Monday or Tuesday before anyone even started to look for him. He was on his own and he knew it now, had to know it and face it and deal with it because there was simply no one at home to miss him any more. And to hell with being missed, he thought. To hell with that and to hell with women and to hell with that goddamned deer, and knew he was so completely lost he might never have to worry about women or deer or anything else again ever.

Mark sat alone on the trunk of the fallen tree in the rain. He stared at the maze of trees surrounding him and did not move, not even when the rain collected in the brim of his hat and began to run down the back of his neck. He sat there staring unfocused at the blur of swamp before him and thought how for the last few years his luck had gone from unbelievably good to unbelievably bad, and how one sledgehammer blow of ill fortune after another had cost him most of his money and then his business until at last, when he seemed unable even to make a decent living doing the same work he had always done, for someone else's money now, he had lost Sheila too, and now he could not even hit a deer at a hundred yards with the same rifle he had once held ten feet over the shoulder of a huge bull elk at four hundred yards while the hungover jerk he was paying good money to guide him through the Canadian Rockies laughed and said, "No way, José," the moment Mark shot but before they saw the bull crumple forward onto its front legs the way a dairy cow kneels and then roll slowly over onto its side. I used to be able to do anything, Mark thought. And now this.

He saw the buck then, looked out through the mist of the steady, slackening rain and saw it standing in the middle of the shallow slough, nibbling acorns from the low branches of a water oak and seeming not to be aware that the man sitting on the log less than four long leaps away was anything that it should fear and Mark, watching without letting any part of his body move but his eyes, knew that truly the deer did not see him, thought Mark was a part of the new-fallen tree because in the rain there was no man-smell and because the buck had long since forgotten the morning's shot and miss and even the running, so that deep in the swamp now it felt safe enough and hungry enough to finish the meal Mark had interrupted with his bad shooting.

Mark raised the rifle's bolt so slowly it seemed not to move and made no sound, drew it back and watched the deer when the bullet clicked up from the magazine, held his breath when the deer looked at him, stared directly at him for a long uncertain moment before it returned to eating. I've got you now, deer, Mark thought as he shoved the bolt home and raised the rifle to his shoulder and fired in one fast, smooth, practiced motion that ended with the kick of the gun's butt against his shoulder.

He did not hear the shot, had never heard any of the hundreds or maybe thousands of shots he had fired at game in his life and for one brief, gut-tightening moment Mark thought he had missed the deer again, had already drawn back the bolt again and seen the empty brass fly past the corner of his eye when the buck looked at him, shook its head with the antlers flailing the air and dipping, then looked directly at Mark, shivered all over, and died. The buck, lying on its side in shallow water, did not even so much as twitch again and the cleanness of the kill made Mark feel good about something he had done for the first time since before the winter began.

The rain stopped at midnight, or rather, when Mark woke and realized the rain had stopped, the faint radium glow from the dial of the Rolex Sheila had given him when they could still afford things made of silver and gold read a quarter past twelve. I wonder where she is, he thought. Lying there under the all but worthless lean-to he had made by placing broken limbs against the trunk of the fallen tree and covering them with cedar boughs and palmetto fronds, then topping all that with the skin of the deer, soaking wet in his rubberized raincoat and jeans, cold, hungry even though he had eaten the deer's liver and heart while they were still warm, tasting the hot, coppery grittiness of the organ meats and feeling so half-wild with the strength the blood had given him that after he had skinned the deer and buried the viscera and hung the carcass over a limb to keep from attracting predators to his camp, Mark cut huge chunks of loin from the deer's back and ate that raw too, because even if he had had matches and could have found some dry powdery shavings in a possum tree or even a pine knot or piece of lighter he knew he could never have found enough dry wood to keep it going; with all that his first thought on waking up alone and lost somewhere within the hundred-square uninhabited miles and more of the Big Bottom at midnight was not of himself or even his children but of where the wife who had left him could be.

Again, Mark wondered why she had gone, asked himself for the ten thousandth time what he could have done or said that made her leave, wondered whether it could have been the money which they had very little of at first and then more than they had either one ever dreamed of only to lose all of it and more in less than two years when the real estate market went to hell, wondered whether it was just that or if all the years of living with him and raising their son and daughter had finally gotten to be too much, whether it had really always been too much, even from the beginning, and that some invisible cord which had held them all together had simply frayed and broken with time. But Mark Perril had no answer, none at all. Not even silence.

The stars were out now. Mark slid out from under the lean-to and looked up at the sky. He drank the rainwater he had managed to trap in his hat since going to sleep and then stood listening to the sound of two owls screeching at each other somewhere out in the swamp. He could see the thin silver sliver of a new moon glowing through the treetops, bright then dark then bright again as huge gold and silver clouds rolled past it. Fallen angels, chased by God, that's what Sheila called clouds like that, Mark remembered, not sheep or pillows or cotton balls but angels, fallen angels. Trying not to think of her though, doing it anyway but trying very hard not to, Mark at last found Orion and let his eye follow the point of the mighty hunter's sword to the Pole Star. He carved an arrow on the tree trunk then, pointing north, so that in the morning even if there was no sun he at least could find the river, and when he had carved the arrow Mark sat with his back against the fallen tree and slept.

Mark dreamt a dream within a dream that night. Or, if life itself is a dream, as Sheila sometimes said, then what Mark dreamt was a dream within a dream within a dream: alternating images of darkness and light beginning with the solid rapping of a gavel on wood and the heavy metal clank of a prison door closing. He was sick too. Guilt overwhelmed him, though he knew of no crime he had done, and in the prison of his dream he dreamt of falling, fell floating backward through a past he did not remember to a woman he had never known. She was very beautiful, and they wandered together through unfamiliar city streets that were as deserted and strange as an abandoned movie set. Once they climbed into the back seat of a parked automobile to make love but a crowd of angry men soon gathered around the car and they had to drive away.

When Mark awoke from the dream within the dream Sheila was standing outside his cell with an oversized skeleton key in her hand and the pictures of two children he did not recognize sewn into the pattern of her dress. "Mark don't come after me," she told him over and over while Mark pleaded with her, told her on his knees that the woman who was very beautiful meant nothing to him, that she was only a dream and he did not even know her name. But Sheila said, "You are lying, Mark Perril. And her name is Time."

In the morning Mark walked to the river. He needed good water and he knew the river, knew that even should he be unable to flag a passing boatman he would surely be within a mile or two of Pineapple Bend, where he could find the old rutted ridge they called the River Road and follow it to the Five Spout Well, where he had left his truck. His luck was running good now too. He found the river in less than an hour and drank his fill of the clean brown water he had drunk as a boy then sat on the muddy riverbank to gnaw the piece of loin he had brought in the pocket of his coat and watch the morning sun flash silver on the ripples the current made where the channel begins to fall away from the bank. The morning breeze had not yet begun to blow and thin wisps of water vapor rose up from the surface of the river the way Mark had seen it rise up a hundred or maybe even a thousand mornings before, and he thought of her, wondered where she could be and why she left and what the dream meant.

Her name was Time, Sheila had said. Time, and Mark remembered fishing with his father on this same river the summer Mark had added a hundred new subscribers to his paper route and won the white-faced, nickel-plated Timex with the black leather strap. It was his first real watch and Mark wore it everywhere, removing it only to bathe and then only when his mother made him. But fishing that day was slow and they had moved several times without catching very many fish until his father, who was a patient man, grew tired at last of his son's constant time-checks and told the boy to stop looking at his watch, that fish bite when they are ready and quit when they quit and that no little round box of gears and springs that some men had the audacity to sell to other men as a means to measure the passing of a man's life or even eternity made one bit of difference to the fish or to him either.

Mark remembered saying then, this before he had ever earned more than ten dollars in any single day or even dreamt of the five-figure commissions he would later learn to make on a regular basis, for a while at least, long before any of that or his first hundred-hour week, Mark remembered telling his father, looking him directly in the eye and saying, "But time is money, Dad," and his father laughing at the thought.

"Time is a lot of things but it's not money, Boy," his father had said then. "But it is all we've got and all you really need to remember about it is that life's too short to drink cheap whiskey." With that Mark's father took a drink from the pint of Cutty Sark he kept in the bottom of his tackle box and smiled, signifying nothing.

No, time is not money, Mark Perril thought. And life is too short to drink some of the rotgut I've been drinking lately. He smiled at that. After a couple of snorts that day Mark's father had begun to elaborate on his personal theories of time and the universe, but Mark had been unable to follow the convoluted reasoning and so had forgotten most of it. He had not understood what his father had said and he did not understand what Sheila had been trying to tell him in the dream, or even why he was wasting time mooning around on a cold riverbank like some lovesick teenager. To hell with time then, Mark thought. To hell with time and to hell with women and dammit to hell with drunken fathers.

He stood up then and began to hurry toward Pineapple Bend, and by not stopping he reached his truck at noon. He had already opened the door too, already drunk his fill of the warm artesian water from the Five Spout Well and was walking back to the truck and unloading his rifle to place it in the gun rack for the ride home: home to no one, to nothing, home only to bathe and change clothes before going to work because time dammit was money in sales if not anywhere else and life indeed was too short to drink cheap whiskey and too short to live alone too, and if he went back now to the eighteen-hour days and hundred-hour weeks he would get the money back and then he would get Sheila back too, because surely that was what she had meant in the dream, that he had not spent enough time working; he already had the rifle's clip in his hand when he looked down toward the edge of the woods and saw the deer standing there, boldly, nibbling on soybeans with its head down and antlers almost hidden, a huge buck that could have been the twin of the one whose heart Mark had eaten, sired by the same sire Mark was certain, and though it was a long shot Mark rested the rifle on the hood of his truck, aimed carefully, and fired.

The buck jumped high in the air, legs flailing, body twisting in mid-air and hitting the ground running flat-out into the darkness where the River Swamp begins. To hell with it then, Mark thought. To hell with all of it, and it was only because he had missed so completely that Mark Perril began at last to know how very lost he was.

Pharaoh's Army Got Drownded

"That's the most dangerous son of a bitch we've ever had in here," Warden Hacker said. He was not a big man, not tall, but he had the demeanor of a bully. None of the three guards standing before his desk doubted, not for one minute, that Warden Raymond Hacker and only Warden Raymond Hacker was in charge of every man, prisoner and guard, who had the fortune or misfortune to find himself within the twenty-odd thousand acres of forest and swamp and field the state perversely called New Canaan Farm.

"Yessir," the tallest guard, a man called Brazos, said. His arms, the color and texture and hardness of the cypress knees that protrude up through the floor of the River Swamp, but thicker, hung at his sides. Warden Hacker once said that Brazos was the only man he had ever seen who could stand at attention and touch his knees at the same time. That was when Brazos received his fourth chevron, a thing as rare among black prison guards in the South in 1968 as black prison guards themselves had been when Brazos finished his tour of duty with the army at Fort Leavenworth in 1959 and came home to apply for a job that even Brazos was surprised he got.

"I want all three of you in here while I'm talking to him," Hacker said. "Son of a bitch got no damn business on a prison farm. Hell, there's white folks sat in Yellow Mama's lap for less than that boy's done."

"Yessir," Brazos said. Yellow Mama was the state's canary yellow electric chair. Brazos liked to imagine Hacker sitting in Yellow Mama's lap: the steel skull cap perched on his bald white head; his arms and little banty rooster legs shaved to take the electrodes.

"Read it," the warden said, pointing to the manila folder Brazos held in his hand, the state penal records of one Harry S. Truman Walker: black male, height 6'5", weight 280 lbs. Numerous scars on upper torso, face, arms, hands. P.O.C.

"P.O.C." Brazos said. It was supposed to mean Prefers Own Company, prison code for a troubled loner: the nonconformist among nonconformists. Sometimes, Brazos knew from the seven years he spent at a maximum security facility, it could mean Plain Old Crazy, but whatever it meant it only got past the prison psychiatrist and into a prisoner's permanent file when the prisoner was or had at any time been considered dangerous to other inmates and potentially to non-incarcerated personnel. "He don't like us," Brazos said.

What Harry S. Truman Walker had done, Brazos told them, looking at the papers in his hands, was draw twenty years to life for killing his girlfriend's husband with a bushaxe. "Choppity-chop-chop," Brazos said, and grinned. When he was stationed at Fort Leavenworth Brazos and some of the other guards had played a game in which each could choose one weapon to take into combat, and it couldn't be a gun. It was a theoretical game, invented to pass the boring long hours, and people chose everything from boarding pikes to machetes. Brazos always chose the bushaxe. He thought he could split a man in half with a sharp one.

"Y'all sit down," Warden Hacker said. He motioned to a row of metal folding chairs along the back wall. They were chained together. Hacker pushed a button under the rim of his desk and a buzzer sounded in the outer office. In a moment two state troopers led Harry S. Truman Walker into the warden's office. As soon as Hacker had signed their papers, the troopers left. Their job had been to deliver the prisoner, cuffed hand and foot but otherwise in good condition. They were through with Harry S. Truman Walker for now.

Warden Hacker and the two white guards were sitting, watching the prisoner stand as completely still and without motion as a tree on a windless day. Brazos was watching him too, but Brazos rarely sat down at work now. He had been sitting down once when a prisoner he thought was harmless walked up and used a knife he had made from a soup can to slit Brazos' left cheek from ear to mouth. Since then the only place Brazos felt comfortable sitting down was at home, alone. But Brazos knew he had a better perspective on the prisoner standing up as well, and even though Brazos was a big man he could see that Walker was bigger, not much, but it could be enough to make a difference. Brazos liked to form his first impressions by whether or not he thought he could take a man in a fair fight, this though he knew that, given the circumstances of his own employment, any fight between himself and Walker was unlikely to be anything close to fair. Barring surprise or stupidity Brazos knew he could take the man.

Harry S. Truman Walker, to Brazos, looked like a man who didn't have either oar quite touching the water but had learned to travel pretty fast anyway: Plain Old Crazy instead of Prefers Own Company. Brazos knew that could make a big difference when the time came, but the only thing he was ever sure of about a man who could hold himself like Harry S. Truman Walker was holding himself now, in this place and under these circumstances, was that the man probably didn't even know what a fair fight was.

"Harry S. Truman Walker," Warden Hacker said then. He was lighting a cigar. "You a True Man, boy?" The warden blew out some smoke. A long gray cloud of it permeated the small office, fouling the air. The warden's cigars were a local product, made of low quality tobacco grown on shares and put together on an assembly line which took up the bottom half of an old shirt factory near Selma and which a young and overly imaginative reporter for a Montgomery newspaper had once dubbed "The Devil's Smokeshop." Hacker smoked the cigars because they were free. His brother-in-law owned the Devil's Smokeshop, Hacker liked to tell people, and although the young and enterprising reporter had failed to stir up any official interest in the cigar plant, Brazos believed some of the tobacco was being grown on state land. This particular batch of cigars though, even Hacker had to admit, looked and smelled like burning dog turds.

"True," Harry S. Truman Walker said. Only his lips moved; his dark face seemed to darken more.

"What?" the warden said. He spit a piece of tobacco onto the floor and placed his cigar in an oversized ashtray on the gray metal desk.

"They call me True," Walker said. Brazos did not see the man so much as twitch; but he could tell he was angry, thought he looked like a man who had been born angry and gotten worse.

"Well, Mister True Walker," the warden said. He thumped the folder on his desk. It was the wrong one. Brazos still had the file on Harry S. Truman Walker in his hand. "This here says you did five years down at Fulman and didn't get suspected of murdering but two of your buddies and beating the living hell out of a couple dozen more, so as a reward for your outstanding behavior and since they couldn't never convict you of nothing on account of a sort of continuous lack of witnesses, the Powers What Be has decided in their infinite wisdom to send you to New Canaan. It's kind of like the old Jimmy Cagney movies, where they send the bad kid out to the country to help straighten him out. Ain't that about right, Mister True Walker?"

True Walker said nothing.

"Well, Mister True Walker," Warden Hacker said. "Just so's we'll all understand one another: It ain't no secret that old man Bishop down at Garrison is the reason you're here in New Canaan instead of pushing up daisies. But I'm here to tell you this: If you so much as look sideways at one of my guards, if one of my prisoners turns up with a black eye he can't explain, hell, if you so much as swat at a skeeter down in the River Swamp, I'll have your ass back in Fulman before the sun sets. And you can use that parole old man Bishop thinks you got coming in two years to wipe your ass. You understand me, Mister True Walker?"

True Walker said nothing. As far as Brazos could tell the man had moved only his eyes and lips since coming into the room.

"I said do you understand me?" Warden Hacker asked again.

"I understand," True Walker told him.

"Brazos," the warden said. There was an edge to his voice now, a meanness Brazos had heard before. It usually meant Hacker was being forced to do something he didn't like, and sooner or later somebody paid for that.

"Yessir," Brazos said.

"You and Sam take this boy over to the shop and get Monk to put some leg irons on him. Tell him I said make them real tight, with a chain so short he can't get his britches down to shit."

"Yessir," Brazos said.

"And Brazos," the warden said, relighting his cigar.

"Yessir?"

"Watch his ass."

"Yessir," Brazos said. Like I'd watch a one-eyed cotton-mouth rattlesnake, Brazos thought as he led True Walker away.

That was July. By September very little had changed. Mornings were cooler, with such heavy dews that walking through the cotton and soybean fields of New Canaan Farm before 9 A.M. would soak a man's pants legs to the waist.

Brazos liked farming, even though he was born and raised in a dirty little ghetto of a neighborhood on the west side of Birmingham. The three-room duplex he shared with his mother and his six brothers and sisters was so near the steel mills that on summer nights when the windows were open Brazos could hear the whistle blow to warn workers that hot steel was being poured. Some nights it woke him. His father, a sullen giant called Little Man Moss, had been killed in a freak explosion that occurred during a pour in 1948, when Brazos was twelve. Water in a ladle, the two white men who came to the Mosses' door at daylight told his mother. Good man, they said. Killed instantly. No, he didn't suffer. That night a man who had been there told Brazos that Little Man Moss had been so big and strong it took him five minutes to die. The man meant it as a compliment, but Brazos never told his mother. He never went to work in the steel mills, either.

But Brazos loved raising cotton. He loved the cleanness of it, loved the raw earthy smell of the fields and the sweet, rich odor of decay that came up from the River Swamp when the wind was right. And most of all he loved not being within a hundred miles of the filth and stench and heat and danger that was all he knew of cities. Brazos hated cutting timber though, which was what they had been doing since the peas and corn were harvested in July and August and what they would be doing until the cotton made in late September or early October. He loved the wildness of the swamp and the big trees there, the hickory and cypress and chinquapin and pine and the dozen different kinds of oaks, but he hated cutting them down and he hated working men in there. The trouble was, you couldn't see. That's what Brazos told the warden. Waiting until December or January, when the leaves were off the trees, would make it a hell of a lot easier for Brazos and the other guards to watch the prisoners.

"Rain," was what Hacker always said, and Brazos knew he was right. September and October and usually most of November were dry in the Deep South. The river was down, so logging trucks and heavy equipment could drive across dry sloughs that would be flooded when the rains came. Anyway, Brazos' real problem was snakes.

"They're everywhere," he told his crew that morning. "Keep your eyes open and watch where you put your hands and feet. If one of these big old cottonmouths or rattlers or copperheads gets hold of you, you'll be D.O.A. at the clinic." Brazos figured that if some of the snakes he had seen around New Canaan, including a seven-foot diamondback that got itself wrapped around the hub of a tractor and bit the prisoner who was driving the tractor in the face when he got off to see what the problem was or the five-and-a-half-foot water moccasin that fell into the boat Brazos was sculling while the warden gigged frogs one summer's night and wouldn't die until Hacker had pumped five shots from Brazos' .357 magnum into it and killed the boat too; Brazos figured that if a snake like either of those ever bit him he wouldn't have to wait to be pronounced D.O.A. at any New Canaan Clinic. He'd be D.O.S., Brazos figured: Dead On the Spot. Heart attack, sure as hell. Brazos would remember later that all the time he was talking about snakes, True Walker smiled.

The early morning was sunny but cool. Brazos knew that wouldn't last long. By ten o'clock it would be so hot you could work up a good sweat just breathing. There was no breeze; there would be none. The river was less than a mile away, but the wall of trees and summer undergrowth kept all but the strongest winds from reaching into the swamp.

Brazos unzipped his windbreaker. He and two white guards were watching a dozen prisoners, including True Walker, clear a road through a cane thicket with machetes and bushaxes and chainsaws. Brazos had only his pistol; the other guards had shotguns. True Walker was in leg irons; warden's orders. Hacker had said from the beginning that the only part of New Canaan Farm True Walker would ever see without leg irons on would be the bottom of a six-foot hole on Burying Ridge, and Brazos knew he meant it. He heard Hacker's Jeep only moments before it pulled into the clearing.

"Good morning, Ladies," Warden Hacker said. He sat at the wheel of his Jeep while Brazos and the other guards walked over to him.

"Morning, Warden," they each said in turn, Brazos first, then the rest of them. Brazos was in charge; he outranked everyone on the prison farm now but Hacker. No one seemed to mind that but Brazos. Not that he minded the job, or even Hacker. Brazos knew that Hacker was more or less just like the rest of them, playing a part he'd had to learn to play on his own and trying to keep any major screw-ups from happening before he retired. He figured that Hacker was neither very much better nor very much worse than any boss he would have had in some other prison or even in some other job. At least you could talk to Hacker. You couldn't get him to change his mind but about once every two or three years, but at least he would hear you out.

No, what worried Brazos, whose real name, Roosevelt Moss, only his mother and Hacker ever used, was what Brazos called the Pharaoh's Army theory. It came from an old spiritual he had last heard sung at his mother's A.M.E. Church in the early sixties; Brazos wasn't even sure what year, but it was around Christmas. The song was called "Oh, Mary, Don't You Weep," and one of the oft-repeated lines was "Pharaoh's army got drownded."

"You done joined Pharaoh's Army now, Roosevelt," his mother had told him after church that Sunday. "But you better remember this: Pharaoh's army got drownded, but Pharaoh didn't." Brazos remembered, too. He thought about it every single day of his life.

"Blacky's going to bring you ten more workers after lunch," Warden Hacker told them.

"Could use some more guards too," Brazos said. A ratio closer to one-on-one would have suited Brazos in the River Swamp.

"Blacky can stay," Hacker said. "Jimbo called in sick and Sam's got to stay in the office while I go to town." Going to town meant Hacker didn't plan to be back that night. Brazos thought Pharaoh had been going to town a lot lately, maybe had himself a little Pharina there.

"Anyway," Hacker said. "They ain't going anywhere. Ain't nothing but a bunch of grifters and dopeheads, except for Harry Truman there. How come you got him using a chainsaw?"

"What else can he do with those leg irons on, Warden?" Brazos said. "He just stands in one place and saws and hopes a tree don't fall on him."

"Well, don't none of you get too close to him," the warden said. "We ain't had a runaway in over three years, and old Harry Truman was born and raised in this swamp."

"Here?" Brazos said. Brazos had somehow gotten the impression that True Walker was a city boy, perhaps because his records said he had been arrested in Mobile.

"Between here and Garrison," the warden said. "His daddy's some kind of caretaker on old man Granville Bishop's place; one owns the lumber yard down there." Brazos had heard the name, but didn't know the man. Trucks from Garrison Lumber Company often came to pick up timber cut on New Canaan Farm.

"We'll watch him, Warden," Brazos said, though in truth none of them had actually stopped watching Harry S. Truman Walker since July.

"And get some trees on the ground, Sergeant Moss," the warden said. "Trucks is coming in the morning."

"Yessir, Warden," Brazos said. Mister Pharaoh sir, Brazos thought, and wished he had one of those sticks like Moses had, one that turned into a snake when you threw it on the ground.

It was mid-morning and hot. Brazos sat with his back to a big gum tree. They didn't harvest gum, it wasn't fit for lumber and burned so slowly that, Brazos' father had told him once, slaves used to cut the largest gum tree they could find to use as a backlog on Christmas Day because they were allowed not to work as long as the backlog lasted, and a backlog from a big enough gum tree could last a week. Makes a good shade tree though, Brazos thought. Man can't expect himself to stay on his feet all day long in this heat. He stood up though, when he saw one of the men who had been clearing brush walking toward him with a bushaxe.

"What's up?" Brazos said. It was Hugh Harris, a.k.a Hugh the Embezzler, a handsome high-roller who had managed to parlay his job as traveling auditor for an insurance company into a lifestyle that included six automobiles, two wives and a missing half-million dollars of company money. Hugh had once told Brazos it took him less than thirty minutes one quiet Sunday morning to program the insurance company's main computer to automatically deposit the rounded-off fractions of cents from thousands of dividend payments directly into Hugh's own bank account, and it took a payment error to an old lady in some place called Winder, Georgia to catch him. Brazos had told him that sounded like stealing money that wasn't even there and Hugh said exactly. The insurance company was willing not to press charges if Hugh would agree to keep the matter quiet and pay back the money. "But who the hell can save any money with two wives and a kid in college?" Hugh the Embezzler had complained.

"You've got to have a talk with Walker, Sergeant," Hugh the Embezzler said. He was leaning on the bushaxe and looked more like a failed sharecropper than a computer expert to Brazos.

"I do?" Brazos said.

"He's dropping trees right on top of us and not saying 'timber' or 'boo shit' or 'kiss my ass' or nothing. Just stands there grinning and watches them fall. He's going to kill somebody in a minute."

"Okay," Brazos said. "I'll talk to him." He walked over toward the tree that True Walker was cutting and when he was ten feet behind the man Brazos stopped and whistled.

"Walker!" Brazos shouted, then he whistled again. The big saw droned steady and loud, kicking a stream of chips and sawdust down at True Walker's feet. If he had heard Brazos, Brazos couldn't tell it and he called again, but still he got no response. The saw droned on, steady and obnoxious. Brazos could see that the tree, a huge red oak nearly sixty feet tall, lacked only inches being sawn through. He stepped up behind True Walker and tapped him on the shoulder.

Surprise and stupidity, that's what Brazos thought. He lay there unable to move, pinned to the ground by the shirtless steel strength of the man he had once decided would not even know what a fair fight was. Brazos did not yet know what had happened; it had been too quick. All he knew for sure was that for one very short moment, which had evidently been quite long enough, Sergeant Roosevelt a.k.a Brazos Moss had been very stupid and as a result had been very surprised.

"Don't want no trouble," True Walker said as he eased himself off of Brazos. Having the wrong end of his own .357 magnum shoved in his face came as somewhat of a surprise to Brazos too.

"Won't get none from me," Brazos said. He stood up and tried to spit, but all his spit seemed to have run and hid.

"Tell the others," True Walker said.

"Man don't want no trouble," Brazos told them. When the other guards did not lower their shotguns immediately Brazos shouted, "Put the damn guns down, fools! You want this man to blow my head off?" They placed their shotguns on the ground then, but only after it had occurred to Brazos and True Walker both that the two white guards didn't seem to care a whole hell of a lot what happened to Brazos' head.

"Throw them in the canebrake," True Walker said. "All of them." He held the gun on Brazos and watched as the guards threw the shotguns into the thick cane. Then he hobbled over to a stump. He made Brazos get a cold chisel from the tool box on the work truck and, with the help of Hugh the Embezzler and a sledgehammer, cut the chains between his legs in two. He did not even try to get the shackles off; that would have taken too much time. When he stepped up to Brazos and put the pistol barrel to his stomach, Brazos heard the chains clink.

"You drive," True Walker said. He shoved the barrel into Brazos' stomach, but Brazos' stomach did not give.

"Hey, man," Brazos said. He raised his hands above his head. "Escape'll get you five. Taking me with you'll get you dead."

"Drive," True Walker said, nodding toward the work truck. He cocked the pistol.

Brazos drove. True Walker sat beside him, shirtless, his back making a wet, slushing sound against the vinyl seat. The pistol on his lap was still cocked and pointed at Brazos. They were on a leaf-covered fire road that ran along a dry ridge toward the river. Brazos thought True Walker seemed to be looking for something. True Walker thought Brazos ought to watch where they were going and quit staring at the gun.

"You know this swamp?" Brazos said.

"I know it," True Walker told him. I was born knowing it, True Walker thought: swamps and woods and rivers and everything that's in them. It's people I can't know.

"He'll kill you," Brazos said.

"Who, Hacker? Hacker's nothing."

"May not be, but he'll kill you. Get you back and put you on a job that'll get you dead."

"Won't never get me back," True Walker said. "Won't never even find me." He meant it. He intended to cross the river and disappear into the swamp and never come out.

"Hell, man," Brazos said. "Blacky's coming. Soon as he calls New Canaan they'll have troopers and sheriffs and dogs and helicopters all over this River Swamp. You got maybe thirty minutes, and that's if Blacky's late."

"Won't never find me," True Walker said. "Not even where I been."

"They caught you down in Mobile," Brazos said.

"Yeah," True Walker told him. "They did." Because he let somebody talk him into giving himself up, he remembered. Old Boss Bishop had sent True a message saying he would help; do it for True's mama and daddy's sake. White man's help; six years later and still wearing chains.

"You mind easing that hammer down?" Brazos said.

"Just drive," True Walker said, but he put the hammer down so the pistol could not fire accidentally. He thought maybe that would shut Brazos up.

"That true about you killing that boy?" What a stupid question, Brazos thought. Of course it was true. You think the man got twenty-to-life for spitting on the sidewalk?

"No," True Walker said.

"No?" Brazos said. Another innocent man. Brazos wished he had a nickel for every innocent man he had met in prison; be a rich man now.

"Not the way they said," True Walker told him. They were still driving along the ridge, but it was more open and the sun seemed brighter.

"Oh," Brazos said.

"I didn't hit him with that bushaxe but once," True Walker said. "Didn't chop him all up or none of that stuff them womens said. Boy just got in my way and I cut his fucking head off." He looked at Brazos when he said that, and grinned. That ought to shut the fool up, True Walker thought.

And Brazos did shut up, for a while. He felt sick and a little dizzy, the way you feel when you bang your head or stand up too fast. He had been seeing the late morning sun reflecting off the river for several minutes, flashing like tiny mirrors between the trees, before he realized what it was. "You going to try and swim that river," Brazos said then. He stopped the truck.

"Drive," True Walker said. He cocked the gun again, but Brazos turned the key and shut the engine off. He'd had enough, would die right here if he was going to die.

"Right there's your river," Brazos said. He nodded toward the brightness in case True Walker had not realized the river was so close. "And even if you're man enough to swim it with those chains dragging you down, all you're going to find on the other side is the biggest and meanest swamp this side of Georgia. This over here ain't nothing. That over there's the edge of the Big Bottom."

"I know it is," True Walker said. He knew it wasn't. It wasn't the edge of the Big Bottom like Brazos thought, but you could get to the Big Bottom by going through it, and True Walker knew if he could get deep enough into the Big Bottom the only man who could ever find him there was Jericho Walker, and Jericho Walker was True's own daddy.

In the silence they heard the deep, throaty rumbling of a tugboat. It was struggling to shove coal-laden barges down-river, trying to stay in the deepest part of the channel. That wasn't always the middle, either.

"Get out," True Walker said. He motioned with the pistol, and when Brazos got out, he got out too.

"You're going to kill me," Brazos said.

"What for?" True Walker said. "Make Whitey have to come after me? Or they come after me if I shoot you? Maybe just say the whole mess your own fault and stick you in the ground and forget it; wash their hands. Save time and trouble and their own asses too. Old Hacker probably rather see you dead than alive right now." Then he grinned again. "You swim?" True Walker said.

"Some," Brazos told him. Brazos could swim just well enough to be scared to death of the river, but he was not about to admit that now. There were all kinds of ways for a man to die, and Brazos had never considered being shot at point-blank range with a gun that could blow a hole through a truck engine to be one of the better ones.

"Then get your shoes off and let's go," True Walker said. "Unless you want to stay here." He grinned again, and they both knelt down to untie their boots.

Brazos swam. The moment they entered the water he heard the wail of the siren atop the water tank at New Canaan Farm and, from the way True Walker turned his head, Brazos knew that True Walker had heard it too.

They swam in near tandem across the river, True Walker with the pistol in his left hand and the shackles on his legs still managing to beat Brazos to the other side. They came out on a narrow strip of beach beneath some water oaks. Their long, leafy limbs stretched out over the beach to the river. While the men were catching their breaths, sitting not more than arm's length from each other and both heaving and blowing and streaming water, True Walker raised his head slowly and looked toward a limb near Brazos' head. Without standing up, and with a motion far too quick for Brazos' eyes to follow, True Walker reached up into the tree and grasped the tail of a big water moccasin which had been lying there and flung the snake into the river. It sunk briefly and then surfaced less than ten feet from shore, treading water with more than a foot of its body held out of the water and its big, ugly head with the tongue flicking pointed straight at them. Brazos couldn't get his breath and thought he was having a heart attack.

"You cornered him," True Walker said then. "That's all. Man ought not never corner a snake unless he means to kill it. Snakes can get real ugly when they're cornered, especially cottonmouths."

"Shoot him," Brazos said. He was watching the snake watch them. It was wriggling like a moving ess and seemed to be inching closer. It sure wasn't backing up.

"He ain't hurting us," True Walker said. "We just cornered him, that's all. Or got in his way. Snakes ain't like people. They won't hurt you unless you give them a reason."

"You like snakes," Brazos said.

"Better than people," True Walker told him. He threw the pistol into the river then and turned to face Brazos. "Don't try to stop me," he said. "Wouldn't want that big old cottonmouth to crawl up here and bite you while we were fighting."

"Might bite you," Brazos said.

"Might not," True Walker said. "I might bite him. He don't know." He grinned again, but the grin faded quickly when they heard barking and turned to see dogs and men standing on the far bank.

"Just let me go," True Walker said then. "I could have killed you."

Brazos looked out across the river. He wished that everything was as simple as this murdering, ignorant, snake-loving son of a bitch seemed to think it was. Good and bad and right and wrong had gotten a way of mixing themselves up inside Brazos' head lately so he couldn't always tell which was which. You didn't save a man's life just by not killing him, Brazos knew that much. A man could save a hundred lives a day if that was all it took. But there was the thing with the snake. That was something, that and what True Walker had said before they crossed the river, about how Hacker would probably rather see Brazos dead than alive right now. Brazos wouldn't have gone that far, it's hard to imagine someone wanting you dead, but he knew damn well Hacker and everybody else at New Canaan Farm would stand by and watch Brazos take the fall for the escape of a dangerous, convicted murderer.

That was when Brazos realized he could never let True Walker go; that whether Brazos could save himself or not, he had to do whatever he could to save anyone who might accidentally happen to get in True Walker's way out there, or corner him. "I've got to try and stop you," Brazos said then, but when he turned True Walker was already gone, disappeared into the swamp; and the swamp had closed around him like a womb.

"Don't you kill nobody!" Brazos shouted after him. He saw a movement in the underbrush, but it was only the wind.

Brazos heard barking and shouting then, and when he turned he saw dogs and a dozen men in boats already crossing the river. Brazos looked at the swamp and he looked at the river and he looked at the sky and closed his eyes, praying that the water would open up and swallow every damn one of them.

The Skinner's Tale

They killed seven deer that morning, which Jericho Walker skinned. Seven nice bucks and a big fool beaver some boys shot when it broke through the ice on Cypress Slough. It was late December too. Past Christmas.

"Leave the cape for a shoulder mount," Dianne Bishop said. Jericho slit the belly of the gambrelled buck with one smooth stroke of his knife. Sleet hissed about them, had since early morning; tiny white specks that stuck briefly to clothing and leaves and the seven hanging deer, then disappeared. Dianne moved closer to the old man, stood directly beneath the stout cedar game pole and spoke into his ear.

"Did you hear me, Jericho?" she asked.

"Yes'm," Jericho Walker said. "A shoulder mount."

Dianne Bishop watched him work with sharp knife and quick, gnarled fingers to open the deer, then cut the viscera free and step back to let it fall into the old and dented tub they called the blood bucket; saw his wide, flat nostrils flare and quiver at the hot, coppery smell. He looked at her then. Dianne knew it was to see if she remembered too. She looked at him closely, but nothing in his glazed and ageless eyes, nor the gray, gaunt blackness of his face betrayed the three-score years and ten, and how many more exactly even Jericho Walker did not know for sure, of living hand-to-mouth and half-brother to every kind of trouble that can come to a man who, Dianne Bishop's grandfather told her once, at least was never quite a slave.

"Can I help you, Jericho?" she asked. Two men and several boys had gathered to watch. They stood leaning against the wide, thick, adze-marked table that Dianne Bishop's grandfather had built into and between the two elephantine live oaks that were big trees already when he and Jericho Walker were boys and now reached toward the gray dark brightness of the winter sky like two brown-leaved mushroom clouds.

These then were the deerslayers, Dianne Bishop knew; those redfaced men and boys breathing short round jets of steam and standing crosslegged and uncomfortable, with hands shoved deep into camouflaged pockets and shoulders hunched against the cold north wind that blew from the river and across the Big Bottom to come to them smelling absurdly of rotting vegetation and high misty mountains, and sometimes even snow.

The others, hunters luckless for that morning and even the lucky ones too cold or too jaded to want to watch their deer being skinned, she knew, were gathered in the screened and stilted camphouse Dianne Bishop's grandfather had built when Dianne was a little girl, with its roof of worn cedar shingles they repaired now yearly and after every storm. She glanced at the old house, saw it standing, leaning into the cold wind and looking gray, yearning toward the river like some drydocked schooner from another time. It seemed huddled almost, about the luckless hunters huddled around her big moss rock fireplace, listening once again to old lies and remembrance, and seemed to shiver with them when the icy fingers of the north wind jutted and jabbed between the clay-chinked cypress logs.

"You can hold the horns up, if you want, while I saw his head off," Jericho Walker told her. Dianne gripped the wide, hard antlers with her soft-gloved hands and lifted the deer's head toward her. Blood trickled from its nostrils when she placed the lifeless, staring head between her knees. She wondered if the house remembered too.

"Don't you get that blood on you," Jericho Walker said. Dianne nodded, then looked at him and smiled. He used those same words, she thought. He can't forget it either. And she wondered why he would not call her by name now. He did when she was a child, until she was grown really, and then stopped suddenly, and in all those years now she had never heard Jericho Walker call any white person by name, until if he had said Dianne to her, or even Ms. Bishop, it would have surprised her as much as if one of the loblolly pines around the camphouse yard or a moss-draped cypress in the Big Bottom had called her name.

"That your biggest deer?" one of the men asked Dianne as Jericho sawed at the thick neck with an old handsaw.

"Biggest whitetail," she said, without looking up. Jericho cut the cape free form the rest of the skin, then freed the head from the body with an easy flick of his knife.

"So the lady's a trophy hunter, is she?" the man asked. Dianne looked to see who he was. She did not know him, except to know that he was the one who had been on the stand next to her that morning and killed the spike that had been running with the big twelve-point she had killed. He had complained too, when Dianne slit the skin between the deer's neck and its goozle pipe, that was what her grandfather called it, and jammed a green limb into the slit and through so they could drag the spike out of the woods, complained as if she were harming the head. Then when he saw her buck already laying in the back of the truck and found out she had killed it, Dianne had smelled the dusty foul odor of male ego burning.

Pete was his name, she remembered, and he had come with her cousin Matthew Perril, the hotshot New Orleans lawyer and first-class prick. Matthew had introduced the man as they stood around the small yard before the hunt, sipping strong black coffee from Styrofoam cups and feeling as much as watching the gray solid dawn lift, until they knew it was sleeting because now they could see what they had been hearing. He introduced the man as Pete Something-Something from Somewhere-Down-South-Now, and him and his boy's going to hunt with us today, Dianne, with that don't-give-me-any-crap-this-is-important stare of his. Some Yankee businessman, she supposed, trying to immerse himself and his family in Southernness just as she and her grandfather had tried to immerse themselves in Africa in 1969.

Dianne remembered the potato-nosed Afrikaner with the thick mustache and teeth like perfectly white ceramic tiles, and she wondered if she and her grandfather had looked as ridiculous to that big wonderful man and the 'Ndrobo skinners and tall, beautiful Masai trackers as Pete Something-Something looked now to her, dressed the way he was in expensive new camouflage clothing that smelled so strongly of newness Dianne thought it could only have been the panic of seeing his big-racked friend killed that had made the spike run within gun range of the man. Her grandfather had said the two of them on safari looked as out of place as a couple of whores in church, but didn't we have one hell of a time, she thought, and now Granddaddy's gone and I'm here hunting with a man he wouldn't have let set foot on his land no matter how goddam important Matthew thought he was, and sent Matthew packing too if he complained.

"Things sure gone to hell around here since Granddaddy died," she said, ignoring Pete Something-Something.

"Yes'm," Jericho Walker said.

"What else have you killed?" Pete Something-Something asked.

"What do you mean?" Dianne said.

"Dangerous game," he said, with an irritating emphasis on the word dangerous. "Besides little Bambi here." He nudged the boy standing beside him. Most of the others had gone into the camphouse. Just Himself and the Son of Heir, Dianne thought. Going to show they don't mind the cold, even if they have to freeze their asses off to prove it. Gameplayers.

Jericho stopped to look at them, and Dianne smiled. She removed her hunting cap and shook her dark hair down about her shoulders, then turned her best smile on the tall stranger and his son. Dianne Bishop at forty-four is not Dianne Bishop at twenty, she thought, but she is by-God still Dianne Bishop and better looking than three-fourths of the women in Garrison, young or old.

The man's face turned a darker red. "I mean like a lion or grizzly or something. You know, exotic. That's what I mean," Pete Something-Something from Somewhere-Down-South-Now said more pleasantly, not weakly.

"I know exactly what you meant, Pete," Dianne Bishop told him. "I killed a buck bigger than this one when I was eight years old. Granddaddy's old L.C. Smith knocked me flat on my butt too, but I killed my deer and I did it with one shot. I've killed a whole bunch more since then too, and a big Cape buffalo they call mbogo that looked like a freight train coming and damn near trampled me, and a silver-tipped grizzly too, Pete. But sorry, no lions, nor elephants either. Is that what you mean?" Jericho Walker was staring at her now.

"I didn't mean there was anything wrong with trophy hunting," Pete Something-Something said.

"Of course you didn't," Dianne told him. "You just wanted to know if I had the guts to kill something that was trying to kill me."

"I guess," he said.

"Well, I don't know, Pete. I honest-to-God don't know. Maybe you ought to ask old Jericho. I've seen him kill the most dangerous animal in the world. Up close too, with that little deerfoot-handled knife he's skinning your deer with. He's not a trophy hunter though. But ask him to tell you about it."

"You mean he's killed a man," Pete Something-Something said. The sleet was falling harder now, stinging their faces. Dianne replaced her cap, then looked at Jericho, who looked at her and his face said why, why now? And she did not know.

"Is that right, Mr. Jericho Walker?" Pete Something-Something asked. "You killed a man with that little knife."

"It were a snake, mister," Jericho Walker said. He stopped skinning the spike to look the overdressed white man in the eye the way Old Boss Bishop had told him to do if anyone ever asked him about it. Snow was falling in big flakes now, sticking to their shoulders and the table and even the ground a little. "That's all she talking about, a snake. It were a long time past, too. Long time past."

Jericho looked at Dianne; and she knew how angry he was, remembered that after it happened he had told her, before anyone else knew, that there was no use ever to tell it, because not the telling nor the screaming nor what anybody did or said would ever make it any better or even any different. She watched Jericho turn from her and withdraw into himself as he had done that day when it was over, and now it was as if she were alone with Pete Something-Something and his Son and Heir in the damp coldness of the early winter afternoon, watching an old black man gut and skin and butcher the deer they had killed that morning as if he were but a machine, or animal even.

The snow stuck to the ground and began to build up on tree limbs and the camphouse roof, and Dianne could see the others now, out and looking, some getting into trucks to head for home, the rest trying to organize a worthless hunt for the sheer novelty of hunting in the snow; but she thought only of her grandfather's words that night, when the sheriff came to ask her grandfather to go with him into the River Swamp and help find Jericho Walker so he, the sheriff, could arrest Jericho Walker for the murder of Jericho Walker's son. Her grandfather had said then, loudly: He did not murder. She heard the sheriff say then, not unkindly: But it was a killing and I am the law. And her grandfather telling, not saying: You are that but you will not find Jericho, then, I will bring him to you in the morning, and you will treat him well.

When the sheriff was gone they had talked. Dianne told her grandfather everything then, and he said so much in reply she could never remember but the few words that stayed always in her mind: At least never quite a slave. Said loudly too, as if her grandfather were speaking to his own grandfather, who had owned men and women as a man owns a cow or a horse but not land, her grandfather told her, because the land can change but never die nor even truly grow old. But his grandfather had owned Auntie, he told Dianne that day, who was Jericho Walker's grandmother, whose real name, Esther Ruth Walker, Dianne saw years later, while visiting her grandfather's grave, carved on a small marble stone in the Bishop family cemetery, back from the river on a knoll they called Graveyard Hill, with the date, April 28, 1887, with "Died Free On This Place," carved below it, and below that, "God Forgive Us."

"I'm sorry, Jericho," Dianne whispered into the old man's ear, but he seemed not to hear her and she knew that Jericho Walker had shut her and the cold and the snow and everything else out of his mind so completely now that he worked freely, as he had always worked, and thought of no future because it did not exist. He had told her that day it did not, that there was only the now and that it was foolish and for the very old to play with even the past. She said but he had saved her life and he said no, it weren't like that, and told Dianne and later her grandfather that if it had not been now then it would have been some other time, and if not Jericho some other man, or woman even, because there are some people and some things that are born just so somebody will have to kill them. They are just plain bad, Jericho had told them. Meaning evil, her grandfather said, but Jericho said no, Old Boss, because if it was evil it would take God hisself to kill it. Not evil, but just plain bad like a man can be bad, and it don't matter if it's your own boy or not, or who, it's you has to kill it.

"Jericho had a son," Dianne said to Pete Something-Something and wished she had not. The Son and Heir had gone to join the snow-hunt. Only Dianne and Pete and Jericho Walker had stayed at the camphouse, beneath the two live oaks. The snow was a half-inch deep and falling hard.

"He killed his own son?" the man asked. They were watching Jericho work. Jericho watched only his own hands.

"I was alone here that day," Dianne said.

"And he attacked you?" the man asked.

"And Jericho came and saved me; slit his throat for what he'd done."

"But it was his own son?" the man asked. "What could he owe you that would make him kill his own son? And you talk like it was some sort of blood sacrifice. I don't understand."

"It were a snake, mister," Jericho Walker said. "And a long time past."

"We buried him in the Big Bottom," Dianne Bishop said. It sounded so simple to her, saying it out loud to another human being for the first time since she had told her grandfather. You didn't say the two of you dragged the bloody and nearly beheaded corpse of a huge black man through six miles of swamp and dug a hole in the soft mud in a place nobody ever went but you, then filled the grave and marked it with nothing because you never wanted to find it again ever, only to have to see each other again ten days later when Jericho was in jail and thank God your grandfather could help him without ever having to tell anyone that the son of Jericho Walker raped you. You don't say that, nor the way you felt when after a year of not coming home it was finally over and your grandfather took you to Europe and then Africa, where you lived alone on safari for eighty-nine wonderful days with your grandfather and only one other white man and twenty-something Masai and Kikuyu and 'Ndrobo, where you learned the simple and beautiful slave trader's Swahili they all spoke. If you said anything at all it would be that without ever knowing exactly when it happened, some time after the mbogo, you were rid of your fear and knew, finally, that Jericho Walker was right; that nothing can ever change it or even make it any better.

You are left then, she thought, with only the puzzle, that here is a man who has killed his own son because of you, or maybe not because of you but because of what that son did to you. A man who told you that if not now, then another time, and if not me, someone else, and meant it. Yet all your life, even when the pain is dulled with travel and too much whiskey and the money your grandfather left you almost all of, and you want desperately to say to the new man you love now, this year, that this happened to me once and I do not understand it. But you don't say that, she thought, and you don't ask Jericho. You don't say: Jericho was it because it was the South, because you knew your son was dead already when he raped me and your knife was the kinder finish? And you don't ask: Who do you blame, Jericho? Because he might tell you, and you do not truly want to know.

"You've been pulling my leg," Pete Something-Something from Somewhere-Down-South-Now said. "That old man didn't kill his own son."

"You're right, Pete," Dianne Bishop told him. "Jericho's telling the truth. It was only a snake."

"And a long time past, Dianne," Jericho Walker said, looking up. "It ain't no need talking about the long time past."